MIRROR WITCH DEMON

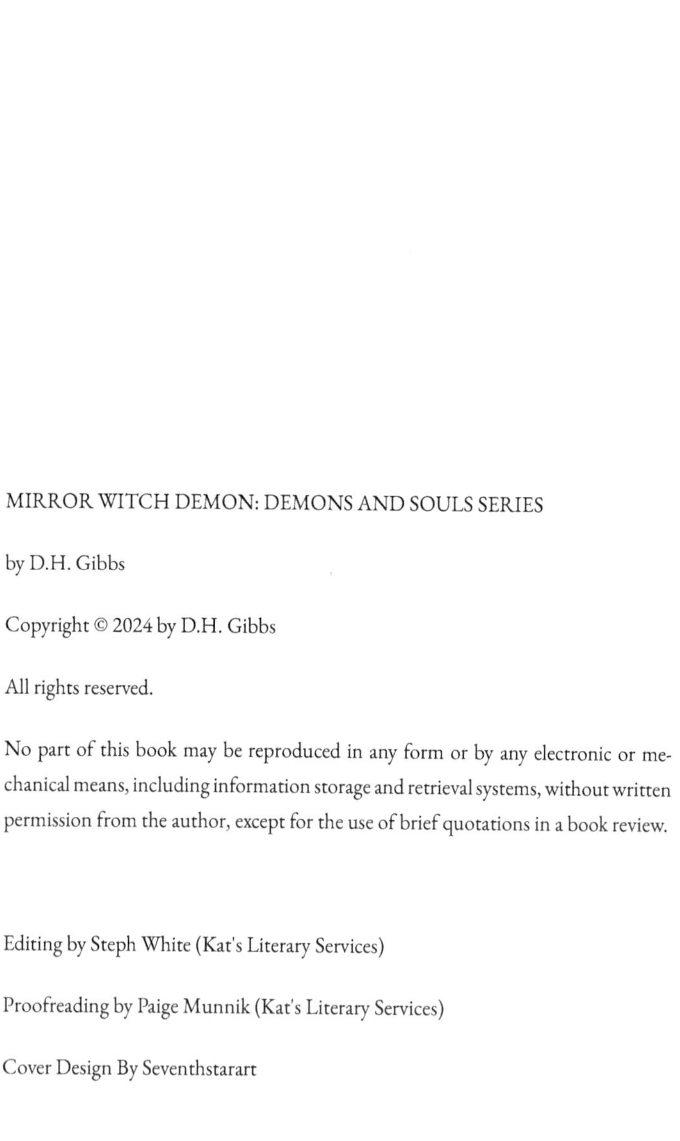

MIRROR WITCH DEMON: DEMONS AND SOULS SERIES

by D.H. Gibbs

Editing by Steph White (Kat's Literary Services)

Proofreading by Paige Munnik (Kat's Literary Services)

Cover Design By Seventhstarart

Contents

For those who see themselves in morally gray characters.

Key Information

T<u>he surface world</u>

Where a multitude of beings live, including humans.

Elysium

The world above the surface world. There are different parts of Elysium, but most who know about the various parts don't share the knowledge. Only "good" and redeemed souls get to live in Elysium, and you can only reach there if an angel takes you.

The Abyss/Underworld

The world below the surface world. There are seven layers in the Abyss.

The Rivers: Ebon Passages. This is the first level, and the river waters lead to the different levels of the Abyss.

Purgatory: Fields of Asphodel. Souls that are not 100 percent innocent stay here until they are ready to move on.

Demon birth level: Amaryllis.** Demons are born on this level. When they die, they don't get separated into the other levels of the Abyss and can't go to heaven. Their souls return to this layer to be reborn. If they're to be tortured, they have to be alive. Abaddon can't torture their souls unless they're trapped in something else.

Punishment of souls level: The pit.** Where all the terrible souls go to be tortured by demons and Abaddon.

Abaddon's level:** Where the king of the Underworld lives and raised his family. The lighting on this level is fake. It is an illusion created by a witch.

Demons' level:** Where the demons build armies, raise families, and form bonds. Demons cannot make their own children, and they form families by adopting young demons when they come up from Amaryllis.

Lucien level:** Where innocent souls go either directly from the Gates of Judgment or after they've redeemed themselves in Purgatory. It is at the top of the Abyss, where the angels collect souls ready to move them to heaven.

<u>Upper-level beings</u>

Witches:** Beings who have similar traits to humans but possess magic of various kinds. They can be killed like humans if their magic can't protect them. When they die, their souls go to the Underworld to be judged.

Demons:** Beings who have a soul but are not born from two beings like witches and humans, but are born on the

Amaryllis level in the Underworld. They are living creatures and eat a variety of food to survive and sustain their magic. Demons are killed similarly to humans or by finding their weak points.

Angels:** Beings created in Elysium to protect "good souls." They don't have a soul themselves, which is why they are so protective of souls. They possess wings that are revealed or hidden away using magic. Like demons, they eat to sustain their magic; however, they only eat natural foods. Angels are celestial and can't be destroyed by anything except another celestial.

<u>Lower-level beings</u>

Creatures that Elysium does not consider worthy of entering Elysium because they are not humanoid creatures. They are a mix of creatures like pixies, dryads, giants, fawns, satyrs, sirens, etc. When they die, their souls cease to exist, and there is no punishment or reward for the life they lived on the surface world.

Chapter 1

The satyr was lying worse than a threadbare rug and a demon who said they didn't make deals.

Selena mentally scoffed at his attempts but waited to see how long he could play it out. She wondered if the creature in front of her, whose eyes had dipped to her chest several times, actually believed he could come into her club, and she wouldn't know what his desires were.

He crossed his hooves, one over the other, the hard keratin clacking as they knocked. Selena's eyes traveled up from the hooves, past the furry legs to the exposed chest, ending on—and she loathed to admit it—the handsome face with dirt-brown eyes. The corners of his mouth tilted up in a slimy smirk.

"Like what you see?" he asked.

"I'll pass, thanks." She looked down at the printed application in front of her as though she didn't already know what was on it. "I see you wish to hire me for a private party?"

"Yes," he said. The smile that had previously died at her comment was back in full swing. "One of my buddies just got into town, and my friends and I want to show him the fun side of the big city."

"I see." Her gaze locked on his. The satyr drummed his fingertips on the table, uncrossing and crossing his hooves once again. "And do you have a location for this… event?" Selena questioned.

"Actually, we were kind of hoping to have it here," he said with a smarmy smile.

"My club?" The words came out as a question, a note of disbelief in her tone.

"Well, yeah. It's not like you use it anymore." He glanced around, taking in the mirrored walls, the cocktail tables, the black-tiled floors, and the spotless bar behind her. "Valaria used to be the hottest club in East End, and you guys just up and called it quits. Not that I'm complaining because now I can use it for a private party, but why did you guys close up shop?"

Selena fought to keep her gaze on the spot in the club that would forever stay with her. The spot that still haunts her dreams, with memories of blood and death.

"We got our club license pulled," she lied.

"That's too bad, but a perfect opportunity for me."

Selena had had enough and laid the satyr's paperwork on the table, drawing a big X through it.

"Thanks so much for coming, but I'm going to have to decline your application, Mr. Thorn. I don't think I can grant the desire you're looking for."

"What?" He pushed to his feet. Anger came off of him in waves, the skin of his upper body flushed a dark red—almost as dark red as the polygon-shaped mirror pendant she wore around her neck. The difference was that he probably always turned red when angry, while her pendant was that unfortunate shade due to a run-in with a demon trying to kill her.

"You can't do that," the satyr said, his hooves tap-dancing nervously over the tiled floor. "I paid the deposit, and that means you work for me."

"That is incorrect, Mr. Thorn." She linked her fingers on the table; her unpolished nails sunk into her palms, while her hard gaze aligned directly with the nervous satyr's. "The deposit you paid was to have this meeting with me so I can ensure you're not wasting my time when I tell you the price I charge for my services."

"Name your price. I can pay it." He crossed his arms over his muscular chest.

"Oh, I know you can pay my price. After all, the money isn't coming from you but from the demons who hired you."

The blood that had previously flushed his body in anger drained out, leaving him pale and a little shaky.

"Did you honestly think I wouldn't know? The moment you walked into my club, your deepest desire was to please the demons who hired you." Selena pushed to her feet, her oversized white cotton blouse sliding off of one shoulder. The wedged heels she wore mirrored the satyr's hooves on the tile. "Tell whichever demon you're working for, my club and my services are off-limits to any of their kind. And if I catch another one of them scheming to use my club for one of their dark rituals, I will personally make them regret it."

"You don't understand," Mr. Thorn said. All the confidence he'd had drained away with the blood from his face, and he was now wringing his fingers. "They're going to kill me if I don't get you to do this party."

She let out a sigh and pinched the bridge of her nose. "I understand that you're in a bit of a predicament, seeing that you made a deal with a demon, but what did you think was going to happen?"

"I thought I could get you to do the party here," he lamented.

"Sorry to disappoint. Had you read the documents I sent you, you would have seen in big, bold letters that under no circumstances do I hold parties here."

"But they said that if you liked me enough, you would make an exception." The satyr was practically wailing at this point, and Selena was becoming increasingly annoyed.

"They lied." She placed her hand on her jutted hip, knowing that in another lifetime, she would never have repeated her next words. "Look, if you need protection from them, then you should go to the council or something. Tell them the demons didn't give you all the details before threatening your life into the deal. I'm sure they could do something."

Thorn scoffed. "The council? You just signed my death warrant, and you're sending me to the useless council for help? The being in charge of the council is a demon—he would never go against his own kind."

Selena wanted to correct him on the demon not helping him, but she'd rather not have anyone know she associated with Raesean.

It was what he wanted, after all.

She gave herself an inner shake, focusing on Mr. Thorn's other comment instead.

"I didn't sign your death warrant, Mr. Thorn. You did when you made a deal with a demon. Everyone in Fusion City knows you never make deals with demons."

Apparently those last words triggered the satyr because he lunged at her, taking her down to the floor with his hands around her throat. Selena didn't hesitate. She released the hold on her magic. It crackled in the air while her eyes slowly changed, the mercury color bleeding over her irises and turning them a reflective silver.

She used the magic to pull the thin slivers of mirrors placed throughout the club to her. The needle-like shards formed a ring around the satyr's throat, slowly digging into his windpipe and spine. She didn't want to kill him, but she needed to make a point.

A few drops of his blood dripped onto her mirrored pendant, and they shined as though she'd just polished them.

"Kill him." The dark thought whispered through her mind.

She fisted her hands, and the shards in Thorn's neck slithered in deeper. Power unfurled within her, and she basked in the euphoric feeling it gave.

The satyr, finally realizing the danger he was in, shifted his hands from her neck to his. Blood gurgled in his throat when he tried to speak, droplets trickling down the sides of his lips. The sight had Selena leashing her magic, and she shoved him away.

She sucked down a few deep breaths before she dealt with the satyr.

"Let this be a lesson to you, Mr. Thorn. Never make a deal with a demon, and never attack a witch in her own domain. Both of them are liable to get you killed."

"Pacco," she called. "Bring me a healing tonic."

Shalik's apprentice popped his head out from the back room where he'd been making and organizing the potions. "Why? What did you do now?"

Selena gritted her teeth at the sass coming from the young potion master. He'd been training with Shalik for over a year now, and he'd taken to everything like a duck to water, including the sass that Shalik always gave her. His only flaw was that he didn't know when to reel it in. Like now, when she had a being dying on her club floor.

"Just bring it," she snapped.

"Alright, alright." There was a clang of glass against glass, and then Pacco began shuffling across the floor. His eyes widened when he saw Selena standing over the kneeling satyr. "Jeez. Isn't he a client? You can't treat a client that way."

Selena rolled her eyes and snatched the bottle from him, handing the potion to Thorn. "Drink."

He took it, swallowing its contents without so much as a thank you.

"Now get out of my club. Next time, I won't spare you." The satyr scrambled to his hooves, stomping hard enough to almost crack the tiles as he walked out the club doors.

Selena glided her fingers over her throat, gently probing the marks the fawn had left behind. The bastard's grip had been strong. Had she not had the foresight to prepare those mirror shards for the meeting, she may not have been conscious to protect herself.

Speaking of shards—she waved her hand to direct them to the restaurant-style sink behind the bar. They fell with a clatter, some of them breaking.

She sighed. She should have just dumped them in the trash and been done with it, but if anyone had gone dumpster diving, they could have used the satyr's blood for any type of ritual. After having too many run-ins with demons, she couldn't chance leaving blood for them to find.

"Where's Shalik?" she demanded, sauntering around the bar to turn on the sink tap, letting the warm water run over the slivers of glass.

Pacco looked at her as though the question was a stupid one. "Where do you think he is?"

Selena swallowed back a curse while using one of Shalik's cleaning potions on the glass. It fizzled as much as her temper at that moment. Her club manager and best friend was going through something, and it was becoming increasingly worrying. But rather than worry, she chose to be angry about it. Anger was a much better emotion than crippling grief, which is what Shalik was fighting against.

Anger didn't help you save Mini, a small voice inside her whispered. She shoved it down deep, as it was a little shit and served no purpose.

"Are you going to clean up the mess you left on the floor? I polished that floor just this morning," Pacco lamented.

Selena inched her head around toward the potion master in training, her anger bubbling to the surface. She could feel her teeth grinding down by the second.

Pacco's eyes widened, and he took a step back, his hands up in an easy-does-it gesture. "Never mind. I'm happy to do it. Not like the club is busy these days. What with all the clients you keep turning down and the club manager passed out from drinking his own potions."

He shook his head as though exasperated with her.

"Sooner or later, those demons are going to catch up with you. You should just invite them to the club. Once they realize there's nothing here for them, they'll head right back to West End."

The flaring of Selena's nostrils had Pacco zipping his lips and scurrying off to the storeroom to grab a mop and bucket. Selena didn't care. She just wanted a moment of peace after meeting a client on her own turf and being throttled for it. Shalik was supposed to have her back. Unfortunately, after a year, his grief had gotten no better like he claimed it would. No, it had only consumed him.

Now, he was nothing but a shell of himself, and she had no clue how to help. The last remaining member of the family who had accepted her off the streets was hanging on by a thread, and she was clueless about how to help him. If anything happened to him, she didn't think she would deal with it... well.

Ducking into one of the cupboards under the bar, she grabbed a mystic bag that she had paid a small fortune to stock in the club. It was supposed to be tear-proof and nullify any residue from magic used so that no one could track it back to the caster. Between the bag and the cleaning potion, Mr. Thorn's blood should be safe. If it wasn't, then he was shit out of luck; she'd done all she could do for a being who tried to strangle her.

He was lucky to be alive after the stunt he pulled. The last guy who tried to kill her didn't fare so well and was probably cursing her name in the Abyss, the Underworld for select souls.

Grabbing the bag and carefully securing the top, she dropped it in the hazardous waste bin.

With a brushing off of her hands, she took two steps from the bar before she felt the vibration of her cell phone in the pocket of her leggings. Sliding it out, she looked at the name flashing on her screen.

Abaddon.

Nope. She sent him to voicemail. Selena had managed to avoid her father for over a year, and she would not entertain him now. She knew exactly why he was calling. She'd reneged on the deal she had made with him, and he was pissed about it.

After all, he was the ultimate dealmaker, and to have someone renege on a deal they had made with him did not bode well for the king of the Abyss. Even if that someone was his daughter.

Gripping the rail, she inched up the stairs to the second level. She could have taken the hidden elevator in the back of the specially renovated building, but she needed to get rid of the anger she was feeling before she confronted Shalik. She was halfway up to the third level when her phone vibrated again.

This time, she paused, her finger hovering over the green button. The butterflies in her stomach practiced the choreography from her favorite classic musical, *Grease*, while she thought about answering the head of the council. She sucked in a breath and hit ignore.

Nope. He was probably trying to reach her on behalf of her father, his boss. They could both suck it. Shoving the phone back into her pocket, she fished her apartment key out and opened the door to her sprawling three-bedroom apartment.

The TV was on, and the news reporter was talking about demons being responsible for the recent uptick in deaths in Fusion City. Selena ignored the report as she crossed the plush carpet toward Shalik's bedroom.

There was a whine and nails scratching the door, her dog Cerberus outside Shalik's room trying to get in.

"Hey there, buddy." She picked up the small bundle of fur, scratching his head while he tried to give her doggy kisses. "Did he ignore you today?"

Cerberus let out another whine like the world was ending.

"Alright, alright. I'll go talk to him, and to punish him, you can chew on his favorite pair of shoes."

The dog let out a sharp bark, and she smiled for the first time that day before setting him on the floor. "Go to your bed," she commanded, and he scampered off to obey.

Squaring her shoulders, she turned the handle of her friend's bedroom door without so much as a knock. The room was almost pitch black, the heavy drapes still shut. She waited a beat as her eyes adjusted to the darkness, and when they did, the anger she'd lost on the stairs returned threefold.

Clothes, shoes, and empty potion bottles littered the floor. It was worse than a house full of unwashed satyrs after five days of partying; it smelled worse too. Then her eyes landed on the man she'd come to see. The butterflies she'd experienced earlier turned carnivorous. Her stomach lurched as she looked him over.

He lay frozen, eyes unseeing, as he stared up at the ceiling.

Chapter 2

"**N**o," she whispered, the horrors of everything that happened a year ago chasing her into action.

Anger forgotten, Selena rushed to the bed where Shalik lay at an awkward angle, one leg hanging off the bed, the other bent at the knee, keeping his upper body on the flat surface. His arms were outstretched on either side of his body as though he'd fallen backward and didn't move after that.

Selena straddled him, her breath trapped in her lungs, her fingers trembling as she reached for his throat. Air escaped her in a rush as she felt the faint thumping that told her he was still alive.

"Shalik," she snapped, patting his face with her other hand, hoping to revive him.

"Come on, come on, come on." The words tumbled over each other like a prayer. She couldn't do this again. Lose another friend, another member of her family. She would absolutely break if that happened.

"Shalik!" she screamed. She slapped him hard across the face. He stirred but didn't wake up. "Shit."

She looked around the room, looking for something, anything, that would help her wake him up. Spotting a bottle of water on his nightstand, she slid off of him and snatched up the bottle.

Her fingers trembled as she uncapped it, pouring the contents on his face. Shalik bolted upright with a gasp. Her knees gave out on her, and she lowered herself to the filthy carpet that, under normal circumstances, would have been spotless.

"Fuck!" he shouted. He shook his head left and right. His once bright blue hair, now as dull as the light in his eyes, scattered water droplets over every surface within range. His gaze landed on Selena on the floor. "What the hell, Lena? Why are you pouring water all over me?"

Selena sat silent as words failed her and she fought to process everything happening.

"Why would you throw water on someone who was sleeping?" he demanded.

His words snapped Selena out of her disbelief.

"You weren't asleep," she whispered, the words like acid on her tongue.

"Yes, I was," he insisted, picking up a random garment from the floor to dry off his face and hair.

She got to her feet, heat climbing up her spine, her magic moving through her as it looked for an outlet to express her anger. "You. Were. Not. ASLEEP."

"Don't tell me what I was doing," he snapped.

"I can very well tell you what I saw, and that's you all spaced out on whatever potions or concoctions you cooked up."

"Oh please," he scoffed. "What do you know about potions? They're perfectly safe if mixed correctly. Which I can do in my sleep."

Selena shook her head, the grief of losing another friend right in front of her eyes sneaking up to choke her. "I may not know about potions, but I know when someone is chasing something they could never have. Just like Lucien chased the feel of my magic, you're chasing that feeling you had with Mini. Now they're both dead, and we'll never see them on the surface world again. You need to accept that and get your shit together, Shalik, or..."

Shalik let out a bitter laugh, cutting off her tirade. "Or what? You gonna cut me off like you did them? Are you gonna abandon me because I'm not doing things your way? Hiding your secret because you won't accept who you are?"

The jab hit home, and she sucked in a breath.

"Do you have any idea what it was like to walk in and see you like this?" she whispered. "You looked dead, Shalik. I walked in here, and I thought you were dead." Her voice cracked on the last word.

Shalik had the decency to give up on the charade and hung his head in shame.

"I'm sorry." He scrubbed a hand over his face. "I just miss her so damn much."

"And you think I don't?" Selena threw up her hands in defeat. "She would be ashamed to see what you've become and hurt to know her death caused you to become this shell of yourself."

Tears welled in his eyes, streaming down his face, but she continued to slip the blade—that was her point—home. "Mini is in a good place waiting for you to join her. Do you think you're going to meet her there if you continue like this?"

"I know." He wiped the tears from his face.

"I can't deal with this anymore, Shalik. You need help. I don't want to walk in to find the dead body of another person I care about. I can't handle it."

She didn't wait for him to say anything else, just turned and walked out the door.

Selena puttered around her room, getting ready for bed. She'd already braided her hair in two and donned her satin cap. Her face was cleansed and moisturized. All that was left to do was to climb her cotton shorts-covered butt into bed. Yet she took another turn around the room, straightening things that didn't need it, ignoring Cerberus, who was contentedly snoring in his doggy bed in the corner.

Truth was, her argument with Shalik still unsettled her. The things he said were rubbing her raw, and she couldn't quite let it go.

Had she abandoned her friends because they hadn't agreed with her about accepting who she was? Should she have kept them closer? Was it because they kept her secret that they died?

Lucien, Mini, and Shalik were her family. She'd chosen them when she'd come up from the Abyss. The four of them had been inseparable in the beginning, until Lucien had become addicted to her mirror magic and she had cut him out of her life. Then Mini decided to work for the council, thinking she could make a difference from the inside. Selena knew they were corrupt, as most world leaders were, and warned Mini about it. Turns out she'd been right.

Now, two of her family members were gone, and the last one was racing to reach them—and in each instance, there was nothing she could do.

She let out a sigh. She was going to save Shalik, whether or not he liked it. Maybe there was an addiction center for potion masters addicted to their own concoctions. She'd never heard of one before, but she was sure there was a need for it.

A soft chuckle escaped her. *It would be just like him to be the first to do such a thing. He was always one to successfully push the limits.*

She walked over to the closet door to make sure it was secured so that Cerberus didn't make a meal of her shoes in the morning. Turning off the lights, she forced herself to climb into bed.

Maybe reading would relax her a little, and she would feel tired enough to fall asleep. She pressed the switch on the bedside lamp and picked up the book she had put on pause a few days ago.

The main character was stupidly entering the demon's den to save her boyfriend, knowing the demon would rip her apart. Before Selena knew it, her eyes were closed, and sleep had taken her under.

Something was touching her. Its fingers were soft and warm as they trailed over her face, lips, then arms. Her eyelids fluttered open, the sleep fog lifting as she stared into the darkened room with a frown.

Hadn't she been reading with the lights on?

Sitting up, she looked around for the book she'd been reading, only to find it on the nightstand where she kept it.

Her heartbeat sped up. She knew for a fact she'd been reading, so how did the book get on the nightstand?

Searching, her gaze landed on every corner of the room until she found him—sitting on what was clearly one of her dining room chairs, legs crossed, pale fingers petting a delighted and comatose Cerberus.

He'd worn a white suit to match his pale skin and hair. All that white on white made him stand out like a beacon in the darkened room. A beacon she had to fight her attraction to.

Her gaze shifted back to her dog in his arms.

That traitor. He was supposed to be a guard dog, not let randoms into her apartment and bedroom. The demon's blue eyes glowed as his gaze raked over every inch of her skin. Casually, she pulled the blanket up so that it covered her budding nipples and he wouldn't see the effect he had on her.

He arched a brow at her movement and smirked.

Whatever.

"What are you doing here, Raesean?"

He placed Cerberus on the ground, and the spoiled bundle of fur whined in complaint. Raesean looked at him, and the dog let out a huff before returning to his bed with a plop.

He linked his talented fingers on top of his knee. "You didn't answer your phone."

"There was a reason for that."

He waited for her to say more, but she remained stubbornly silent. Finally, he caved and asked, "What was the reason, Selena?"

"I didn't want to talk to you." She gave him a saccharine smile, and a muscle in his jaw ticked.

"Did you stop to think it might have been important?"

"No, I didn't. Besides, you're the biggest and baddest demon in Fusion City, and you run the council. I'm sure whatever it is, you can handle it."

He stood, walking closer to the bed, eyeing her for a beat before he slid his hands into his pockets. "Have there been any demons around the club lately?"

She frowned, wondering where this line of questioning was going. "No. You know I maintain my no-demon rule, and none of them can pass the vestibule of the club. Their desires are always dark."

Before Selena shut down Valaria, she and Shalik ran a nightclub that granted people's desires. She would use her mirror magic to tell if their desires would cause harm, and if they would, the doors would automatically lock them out. Many demons didn't appreciate the way she kept them out—and still didn't, if the satyr's appearance was any sign.

At the thought of the satyr, she ran her fingers over her neck, hoping the bruise left behind wasn't bad.

Raesean tilted his head, one hand darting out to grab her wrist, the other conjuring his fire magic. He held the small flame up closer to her throat. She froze, knowing that one stray amber of his Abyss fire magic could light her up in seconds.

"Who did this to you?" he demanded, snuffing the flame out when his fingers closed into a fist.

Selena tugged her wrist out of his grasp. "What does it matter, and why are you even here?"

As though realizing what he was doing, he took several steps away from her, shoving his hands back in his pockets. "There have been reports of rogue demons in Fusion City, but I haven't been able to track them down."

"And you want to know if I've seen them?"

He gave a Gallic shrug.

She narrowed her eyes at him. The demon was hiding something, and she knew it. "Why haven't you been able to track them down? Every demon who comes to Fusion City has to come to you first. You are, after all, Abaddon's right-hand demon and the demon representative on the council."

The council comprised three heads to represent all of the creatures who lived in Fusion City—a human to represent humans, a demon for the demons, and a witch for everyone else. Now there were only two representatives, as the last witch had turned out to be a genuine piece of work. They should have replaced her months ago, but the witches can't stop fighting among themselves to select a replacement.

"Are you implying," Raesean said, cutting into her thoughts, "that as council, I should be all-knowing?"

"I'm not implying anything. I know if these demons had visited you when they arrived in the city, then you should have their blood donation to give to a scry witch."

"I said they were rogue demons. Never said they belonged to me."

Icy fingers of fear slithered up her spine. "If they don't belong to you, then where did these demons come from?"

A muscle in his jaw ticked. "Have you spoken to your father recently?"

Selena looked away. "Why would I do that?"

She heard the soft padding as he moved further away from her. There was a creak, and she looked back to see that he was settling in her dining room chair.

"Your father has been trying to reach you for several reasons. One being you made a deal with him, and you broke your bargain."

Selena rolled her eyes, ready to launch into all the reasons why her deal with her father wasn't any of his business.

"The other reason," he went on, "is that the rogue demons we're searching for are looking for something. Or maybe some-one."

"You think they're looking for me? Why?"

"I don't know for certain, but after the last demon we went head-to-head with, I hope we never find out."

Chapter 3

Someone had left their mark on her neck.

Raesean thought back to the dark bruises around her throat. The distinctive finger indentations that weren't marks of pleasure but ones of pain. Whoever it was tried to remove her from his world, and that someone was going to suffer a great deal for it.

He slipped into the back seat of his car and jerked his chin at his driver, Henry. The Sacrodaemon, a special type of demon who lived to serve, started the car. He pulled away from the front of Valaria and out into the empty city streets.

Raesean looked out the window, watching the late-night partygoers and stragglers walking the sidewalks or trying to hale cabs before the sun came up. The typical view on his way to the Lower West Side did nothing to calm the rage that was racing through him.

He slid his cell phone out of the inner pocket of his white tailored suit jacket. He pushed a button; the call connected to one of the demons he had on rotation, watching Selena day and night.

"Yes, boss?"

"You left a few things out of your report?" Raesean said. His voice was low, and the demon on the other end of the line knew he was pissed.

"No, I didn't," the demon rushed out. "The satyr was only there for like thirty minutes and walked out fuming. When we checked, she was fine, not a scratch on her."

"That isn't exactly true. There is indeed a scratch on her." His voice was menacing as he fought the urge to hunt down the demon on the other end and eviscerate him.

"Boss, I swear," the demon begged. "The pixie we used to check on her said she was fine, and she'd been arguing with the young potion master."

"You used someone else to check on her?" The phone in his hand creaked as his grip tightened. Raesean had to force his fingers to relax lest he break it before the call was over.

"Yeah, boss. We had no choice. We can't enter her club because us demons have dark desires, and the doors are spelled to lock us out. So we had to let the pixie sneak in when the satyr stormed out."

He paused, turning over the demon's words. Selena's spelled vestibule was both a blessing and a curse. It stopped one who wished to harm her from getting in, but it also stopped anyone who wanted to help. Not like the demons wanted to help. They were just following his orders and knew they would get a fiery ticket back to the Abyss if they failed him.

"Pick up the satyr and bring him to me tonight," he instructed.

"Sure, boss. Right away, boss," the demon babbled, and he cut him off with the push of a button. The sky was lightening on the horizon. Raesean felt the sharp edges of exhaustion after working a full night at his club and then his impromptu visit to Selena, but he couldn't go to bed yet.

No, he had a meeting with a satyr. A long, slow, torturous meeting. For the satyr, not for him, as he would sleep well when it finished.

The smell of coffee curled around her, luring her from sleep like a fish on the line, and she willingly went. Her eyes fluttered open, the sandy feel of it a reminder of the restless night she had had, with a demon showing up and all.

She pushed up to her elbows, breathing the smell in deeply, even though she'd never drink the stuff. She preferred a strong cup of tea in the morning, and if she drank coffee, it was one of those fancy, overpriced lattes from the coffee shop around the corner.

Selena hadn't woken up to the smell of Shalik making coffee in a long time. Months, in fact, and she was wondering if it was him or if Raesean had come back to annoy her and was helping himself to her kitchen.

The choice between going back to sleep and waking to see what was happening wavered within her until the fatty scent of crispy bacon mixed in with the coffee, and then all bets were off. Flinging back her covers, she hurried to relieve herself in the bathroom, brushed her teeth, and then rushed to the kitchen. Shalik was placing cooked scrambled eggs next to the bacon on a plate.

"Tea?" he asked. Her favorite mug that said "demons can suck it" was already in his hands, waiting.

"Yes, please."

She eyed him as he placed a peach-flavored tea bag in the mug, pouring hot water over it. He looked more like his old self today. He'd colored his hair back to the vibrant blue he favored.

His honey skin wasn't as ashen as it was when she saw him yesterday, and his brown eyes were focused, aware of what was going on around him.

"Sit," he commanded, pointing to one of the dining room chairs before placing the plate and tea in front of her.

"Thanks." She grabbed the fork from the table and scooped up a bit of the eggs, savoring the fluffy bite. "Humm."

"I've decided to get some help," Shalik blurted out.

Selena paused at the next bite of her food. "What kind of help?"

"I'm going to an addicts anonymous treatment center, then I'd like to resume managing the club's affairs."

"Oh." Selena swallowed the emotion that clogged her throat.

"That is if you want me to. I know I haven't…"

"Please, yes. You know I hate doing the books and record-keeping. And your protégé is a little shit."

Shalik busted out a laugh, and her heart jumped with joy at the sound.

"He is, but you can't have anyone without an attitude around you because you'll just trample all over them."

"What's that supposed to mean?"

Shalik cocked his head at her. "Selena, even your dog has an attitude."

They both looked over at Cerberus in his cage, and the ball of fluff huffed as though he understood what they were saying. To be fair, he probably did.

Selena's eyes met his, and the pair burst out laughing.

"You're probably right." She shoved more eggs in her mouth, then moaned at the crispy bite of bacon she took.

Shalik turned on the TV, and the news reporter droned on about more rogue demons who were killing people in Fusion City. "Do you think they'll catch them soon?"

She shrugged her shoulders. "I don't know, but I don't want to get involved after the events of last year."

They both paused, thinking about what happened last year. The bodies they found in this very club, one of them being a close friend.

Shalik shook his head as though to dislodge his thoughts before taking a bite of his food.

Selena listened to the story a little longer, sipping on her tea. She didn't want to get involved, but after last night's visitor, she knew she already was.

The next week, Shalik showed her he was definitely on the mend. He'd resumed his duties as club manager—reviewing the books, taking stock of the goods they had, and organizing appointments.

Since they'd silently agreed never to open Valaria again, they opted to do private parties instead. Selena would use her magic to find out what people's desires were, and he would concoct a potion to temporarily grant them their wishes.

Though a year ago, many thought she was the five-hundred-year prophesied mirror witch who could permanently grant someone's desires. Thankfully, with a little water magic, Fusion City has her listed as a mid-level mirror witch. Not the high-level mirror witch she really was.

It was a good thing, too, because her magic didn't grant wishes and transfer power like everyone hoped. No, her magic took souls, and she doubted anyone would be happy if they came to her for their ever afters and she sent their soul to the Underworld.

Nope, if they found out, she'd be lucky if they only burned her at the stake like witches of old.

So, she stuck to granting temporary wishes with the help of Shalik's potions. And the good part about doing this business was the large amount of money they could charge for their services. Nobody else but her could truly extract what someone's desires were, and Shalik was talented enough to whip up a potion quickly to grant them their wish.

The downside of doing private parties, though, was that she didn't have her spelled vestibule to lock out anyone with unsavory desires. Which, unsurprisingly, mostly came from demons. Demons who were right now flooding the party they were hired to do.

Her gaze slid over to Shalik, who was setting up his table that would house all the ingredients for his potions. The chicken burrito she'd eaten earlier this evening turned to lead in her stomach.

He'd lasted one week.

One week before he'd fallen back into the mixture he used to numb his pain. The sheen of sweat on his forehead and the red, glazed eyes gave him away. Shalik was deep in the effects of his potion, or he was coming down off of it.

Either way, the timing for him to fall off the wagon was terrible. The demons currently sipping on their drinks eyed them like freshly slaughtered lambs. Selena laid a hand on Shalik's arm, plastering a smile on her face.

"Are you okay with doing this?" To anyone who was looking at them, it would seem like they were having a pleasant enough conversation.

He swiped the back of his hand over his mouth. "Yeah, why?"

"It's just that you seem a little out of it."

"If you have something to say, just spit it out," he snapped.

Conversation quieted, and Selena forced her smile to brighten. Some demons had the power to use anger and fear as weapons, and she didn't want to give them ammunition to be this evening's entertainment, or worse. Rather than escalate the conversation into an argument, she took another approach.

"I thought this was supposed to be a birthday party for a dryad? Why are there so many demons here?"

Shalik looked around as though only now noticing the predicament they were in. "It was. The lady I spoke to on the phone said her daughter was turning sixteen and wanted us at her party because her daughter and her friends love us."

"On the phone?" The lead burrito was now sizzling and eating the walls of her stomach. "You didn't interview her at the club?"

"No, she said she couldn't make it across town for the arranged time, and that she would triple our rate."

"Are you…"

"Is everything alright?" Selena looked over at the female who interrupted them. There was no way in the Abyss that she was a dryad. She wore black-heeled, knee-high boots, a red corset, and what looked like a lacy black thong. Selena couldn't be sure until the female turned around.

She knew a demon when she saw one, and this was definitely one. A female one. Which was worse than dealing with an upper-level demon like Raesean.

Shit. They'd been played.

Female demons were rare and usually confined to the Abyss by her father because they tended to be vicious and batshit crazy. A combination that proved to be lethal for humans willing to cooperate with the supernatural world.

The demon cocked her curvy exposed hip, reminding Selena that she'd asked a question.

"There seems to be a discrepancy in the application form for this party. We were told it was for a dryad teenager and friends, not for half the demons in Fusion City."

The smile that tugged up her face was anything but warm and welcoming. More like a piranha eyeing its next meal. "Isn't that a pickle you've gotten yourself into, Selena?"

Selena rolled her eyes. She'd had enough. "Let's cut the bullshit. You've obviously gone to a lot of trouble to get my attention. I'm assuming you're responsible for the satyr and the litany of creatures trying to use my services over the last month."

She felt Shalik shifting beside her, probably now realizing the danger they were in. If they made it out of here alive, she was going to kill him. "Now, what do you want from me...?"

"Lima," the demon supplied. The other partygoers had given up pretending to be here for the party and had set down their glasses to watch the show.

We're screwed.

"What do you want, Lima?"

She took a step forward, hips swaying, boots clicking on the tiled floor.

"Just a bit of information. It came to my attention that last year, there was a series of murders in your club, and the being responsible was caught."

Double shit.

According to the media, the being responsible had not, in fact, been caught.

Only a few knew the demon had had his soul ripped out and sent to Abaddon to be tortured. Because he'd been a very naughty boy with plans to overthrow the ruler of the Abyss.

"I didn't realize they caught the person. I thought the investigation had been ongoing." Selena stalled. She felt Shalik touch the back of her hand, and she relaxed the fingers she hadn't known were folded into fists. The flat, cool surface of the circular disk he slipped into her hand was like a balm to the shock of nerves that were running through her blood.

Her magic purred within as she ran her thumb repeatedly over the mirror. She needed to feel every crack and flaw in it so that when the time came, she could shatter it into shards aimed right at Lima's neck. Something she knew she only had one shot at.

Hopefully, when the demon was down, she and Shalik could escape. If not, she was going to have to unleash the full wrath of her magic and take out every demon in this room, or the secret of her abilities would be all over Fusion City in a heartbeat.

Demons were horrible gossips. She had been through too much to keep the level of her magic a secret. The last thing she needed was everyone on her doorstep making demands for things they didn't know about.

Lima took a step closer. Her voice sounded more like it should be in the bedroom than here, making threats. "I can't believe not one demon has figured out who you are. They should have already dragged you back to the Abyss for your disobedience. But your father has always been soft on you."

She leaned in close enough so that Selena could smell the faint whiff of her lilac perfume. "I know you're responsible for sending my cousin's soul to be tortured. You could have just let him return to the Abyss; instead, you trapped his soul with your little glass and sent him to Abaddon. Did you know Abaddon had his dogs rip my cousin's body apart?"

"You're speaking in riddles, and I don't know what you're talking about." Selena stepped back to re-establish her personal space, but the demon kept coming.

"Did you do it alone, or did you have help?" she demanded.

"You need to explain what your problem is because I don't know what you're talking about." Selena stuck to her guns, even though it might have been a wasted endeavor.

Quick as a viper, the demon reached out and snagged Selena's hand, squeezing until the mirror in her palm broke. The sharp shards dug into her palm as Lima used her demon strength to stop her from opening her hands.

"You're such a weak thing with your little mirrors. You can't even do anything with your powers once your mirror is broken."

Selena ran her tongue over her bottom lip. "I see you and your cousin got your information from the same place. And just like him, you know nothing about my magic."

The original plan to take out only Lima had dripped to the floor, along with the blood from her hand. So Selena let go of the tight rein she had on her magic.

Chapter 4

The demons were screaming, and their screams beckoned the deep primal magic in her blood.

All the anger she'd felt over the last year, all the hurt and pain, unleashed as she shattered every reflective glass surface and used it to slice into the demons.

Lima had tried to use her unnatural strength to break her arm, but Selena had forced the shards in her hand to slice through her palm into Lima's. Lima squealed like a stuck pig.

So much for me being weak.

She writhed at Selena's feet while the glass shards burrowed under her skin and up her arms—a sharp parasite searching for the best place to do the most damage. If Lima was lucky, it would quickly nick an artery, and she would bleed out. If not, she would have to wait until it reached her heart.

Banging on the walls and door shifted Selena's attention to the other demons trying to get out. Some had even mustered up the courage to attack her. Those were the ones she swiftly dealt with. A quick slice across the throat, wrist, or tendons in the ankle incapacitated them enough.

Who could chant or throw magic at her with their throats torn open and their wrists hanging on by a slice of skin?

Selena's gaze roamed around the room.

"So many souls ripe for the picking," the dark voice inside her whispered.

All of them caught in their own web. Lima had chosen this place well, with no windows and one door. It really was a great way to trap someone—or, in this case, fifty or so demons.

Unfortunately, if she'd wanted to corner a mirror witch, she should have used paper cups at her party. Her cousin had been smarter; he'd used a pit when he'd tried to capture her.

Stems from champagne flutes and chunks from broken scotch glasses flew, embedding themselves into the necks, eyes, and soft parts of the demons. Her blood sang with joy with every drop of blood that fell to the tiled floor.

"Selena!" Someone was calling out to her, but she ignored them as more and more of the demons felt her wrath.

The mirror pendant around her neck floated up, and, with a pulse of her magic, it separated into tiny fragments. She directed the fragments to circle the female demon before pulling more magic to send a bright white magical light from her body to reflect off of the tiny specks.

In the past, she'd had to crush her pendant by hand, but ever since her run-in with Lima's cousin, the pendant would fall apart and reform at her will. The new trick was handy in situations like this.

"Selena, stop." That annoying voice was back again, this time with a hand on her shoulder. Selena held firm, continuing to torture the demons, especially the one wriggling at her feet.

Lima had come here to punish her for her cousin's fate, only to end up in the same predicament as him. The irony in the situation was beautiful.

Pulling the broken mirror shards from Lima's body, she brought them together until they almost made a perfect circle once again. Selena lifted the mirror so that it was eye level with Lima. All she needed was for Lima to look into the mirror.

The sudden banging of the door against the wall had Selena glancing at the exit. She couldn't allow any of the demons to escape. They'd seen too much, heard too much, and she didn't want people to know how strong her magic really was. She didn't want everyone to once again believe she was the prophesied mirror witch who could grant them powers.

Her eyes met those of familiar pale blue ones.

"Is this a private party, or can anyone join in?" Raesean asked, stepping into the room. His hands slid into his suit pockets while he took in the destruction she had wrought. "It seems you've let your temper take control, Selena."

"I don't know what you mean." Selena turned back to Lima, ready to finish what she had started.

"Since when do you use your magic so carelessly? Anyone within a ten-mile radius can feel the magic you're using. Are you finally ready to show the world who you are?" he asked. Glass crunched under his shiny shoes as he crossed the room toward her.

Her brows met as she thought over his words. Was she being careless and revealing the truth of her magic to others? That was dangerous.

"Selena." The voice that had been calling out to her in the heat of the battle dropped a hand on her shoulder. She looked up into the brown eyes of her best friend—her family—and felt the heat of battle drain from her.

"Are you okay?" Shalik pulled her into his arms, squeezing tight, and Selena released her control on the glass in the room. The shards crashed to the floor. Some of them shattered on the tile floor, while others impaled the demons on their way down. Many groaned in renewed pain. She didn't care.

Burying her face in Shalik's chest, Selena tried to remember what had come over her. Something had gone very wrong, and she wasn't sure exactly what.

"Now that you're back to that part of yourself..." Raesean's voice cut into the moment, forcing Selena to pull away from Shalik. "Why don't you let me take care of these pesky rogues?

You should leave before anyone else comes looking to see what happened."

She looked at him, questioning the anger in his eyes but not having the strength to ask him about it. Instead, she just nodded. Grabbing Shalik's hand, she pulled him out the door. Before they'd even made it down the stairs, the demons' screams started up again, and the smell of burned flesh followed in their wake.

Flames danced over Raesean's fingertips as he walked through the blood and glass on the floor. His shoes sounded like he was walking on sandpaper with each step he took. Whenever he came to a demon who had already returned to the Abyss, he dropped a spark on it to ensure nothing of the body remained.

He chuckled to himself, glancing around at the carnage. Selena might think she's above the demons, but she has a temper just as bad as them. After he made a round of the room, he returned to the female demon who'd led this silly revenge party. Lima was still writhing on the floor where Selena had left her.

The bitch was lucky Raesean had shown up when he did, or her soul would have gotten a one-way ticket to the Abyss straight into Abaddon's hands. A fate worse than death if he remembered correctly from watching the king of the Abyss work.

Raesean squatted next to the female, waving his flamed hands in front of her face. Her gaze locked onto his, and she whimpered at what she saw there.

"What are you doing in Fusion City, Lima?" he asked.

She sucked in a breath, and Raesean could practically see her steeling her spine. "I thought it would be a nice place for a vacation. See the sights, have some food, meet some old friends."

He lowered his hands closer to her face. It was turning a bright shade of red now to match the corset that she wore.

"I'll find out, one way or another, what you were doing here, but trust me when I say it'll be easier if you tell me. Then I can send you back to the Amaryllis level in the Abyss. You can spend a few decades down there, trapped in the dark, until your soul is strong enough to make a body that can return to the surface. Then you can be back to your regular old self again."

"Just send me there and be done with it," she spat.

"You're missing the point. I'll only send you there if you tell me what I want to know."

Lima laughed. "I'll never tell you. So you might as well start the torture then."

"You're right. I'll just get Selena to bring in her mirror so she can send you to her father. You know she's been looking for a gift to give him for Father's Day."

Lima's eyes widened, and her tongue darted out to coat her lips. She tried to push herself up, but the glass Selena had slid under her skin and up her arms had done a number on the muscles and tendons.

The princess was vicious.

"Anyway, I'll see you on my next visit to Abaddon. Who knows, he might even let you see your cousin. Wouldn't that be a treat?" He moved as though to stand.

"Wait," Lima said, "I'll make a deal with you."

"I'm listening."

"Let me stay here at your side, helping you run the demons in the city, and I'll tell you everything you want to know."

"That's a very lucrative deal you'd like to make. Tell me who sent you up here, and I'll think about it."

Her throat bobbed as she fought the pain in her arms, pushing herself upright. "It was my father, Belial. He sent me to avenge Alden. He was like a son to him."

"I see," Raesean said. "Anything else you'd like to tell me?"

The muscle in Lima's jaw tightened. "I'm not telling you anything else until you agree to our deal."

"It was worth a shot," he said with a sigh. Standing, he used his flame-free hand to brush imaginary lint off his suit. "I'll see you in the Abyss, Lima."

"What? Wait, no!" A blue spark fell from his hands before she could say anything else, engulfing her in the hottest flame from the Abyss.

Raesean didn't wait to see her burn. Her shrieks were enough for him. He walked around the room, looking for another demon who could give him more information. Demons were notorious gossips. He was sure someone else could tell him what she was unwilling to.

He found his prey trying to sneak his way out the door, dragging his useless legs behind him. Selena had really done a number on these demons in here.

"Well, hello," he whispered, waving his flamed hands in front of the demon's face. "Now tell me what you know."

"The wraith," the demon whispered.

Raesean smiled as the demon trembled before him. Gosh. He really missed the torture he'd meted out while in the Abyss. He really must make trips back more regularly.

Getting the information that he needed hadn't taken as long as he'd thought. After he'd burned the last body, removing any trace of what happened, he left through the back exit of the building.

Raesean climbed into the back seat of his car, the leather groaning as he settled himself.

"To Selena's," Raesean said to his driver, Henry. The Sacrodaemon, a type of demon who lived to serve, nodded. He turned the engine over, then eased out of the alleyway behind the building.

Raesean looked down at the sleeve of his white jacket. There was a spot of blood on it, right on the edge of the cuff. His gaze traveled over the rest of the jacket, and he found other small flecks in a myriad of places.

Another suit ruined.

"Change of plans, Henry. Take me to my place first. I need to clean up."

The demon nodded again. He never spoke, never questioned—just nodded and followed his orders. It was why he'd hired him for this position. He needed someone who would remain silent, no matter what he heard, and who better than a demon who wouldn't speak?

The car pulled into the garage of his apartment building. "Wait here. I'll be back shortly," he ordered.

It took no time for him to let himself into his private elevator and watch the numbers climb to his condo, which took up the entire floor. He didn't examine the reason he wanted to get cleaned up before he saw Selena. After all, he was the one who decided not to pursue anything further.

How could he when she was the daughter of the man he was indebted to? The man who'd saved his life more than once. The last thing he needed was to get involved with the one creature whom the ruler of the Abyss would burn everything down for.

No, he wouldn't think about why he wanted to look his best before he saw her. Why the blackened muscle some might call a heart gave a squeeze every time she was near. He would go to her, let her know what he found out, and then they could talk about what the hell had happened with her magic today.

Crossing the unfurnished living room to the bedroom, Raesean stripped off his jacket and shirt. He dumped them in the dry-cleaning pile and was about to remove his pants when he heard it.

The croaking of a frog.

He turned around, following the sound back to the center of the living room, where the amphibian waited patiently. Its gigantic eyes looked him over, throat swelling with each of its croaks.

Raesean brought his hell flame, tossing a spark on the frog. It went up in flames, turning to dust instantly. Smoke rose from the ashes, forming into the shape of the king of the Underworld.

"You could have just called me on my cell," Raesean said, folding his arms over his bare chest.

"That's no fun," Abaddon said. His shadow form walked the circumference of the painted portal circle he used to travel from the Abyss. Abaddon took in the empty room with heavily draped curtains that covered the floor-to-ceiling windows. "You really should furnish this lovely apartment. It's dreary, isn't it?"

"Why bother? I'm hardly here anyway. I spend most of my time at the club."

"At least there's that. This place looks worse than a torture room in the Abyss." Abaddon tapped a finger against his chin as though he was thinking about adding his empty living room to torture souls in the Abyss.

"To what do I owe this plague visit and not a phone call?"

Abaddon lost all forms of playfulness as he turned to him. The king was in his presence. "The demons are getting restless down below. They're fighting against the invisible toque around their necks, hoping to gain freedom to the surface world."

"You and I both know that many of them don't even know the meaning of freedom. They just want to thrive on the chaos they'd cause. I've had to increase punishment for those pushing the line."

Abaddon tugged on the sleeves of his suit jacket. "They're testing me, Raesean, and I don't want to destroy half of the demons in the Abyss because of a few rogue ones."

Raesean scrubbed a hand over his smooth chin. "What if it's not just a few rogue demons?"

Abaddon's eyes went hard. "Tell me exactly what you know."

Chapter 5

Selena sat on the sofa, her hand freshly bandaged and feet curled under her as she suffered through various channels for news of what happened. So far, nothing had been mentioned, but that didn't mean that it wouldn't be.

Her hair was still damp from the shower she'd taken earlier, and the two braids she put it in dripped onto the white cami and booty shorts she'd put on.

The TV clicked as she changed the channel again.

"Anything?" Shalik asked. He settled himself on the other end of the sofa in black sweats and a sleeveless T-shirt.

"No," Selena muttered, still pissed at him. It was because of him they were in this mess. If word got out about her magic, she was going to have to pack up and move, or else every being who wanted to use her magic would soon knock on her door.

Shalik sighed, and Selena continued to ignore him.

"You have every right to be mad at me."

She slammed the remote down on the glass coffee table in front of them. "What exactly should I be mad about, Shalik? That you broke the rules and took an interview over the phone? We decided to use the vestibule for our own safety. You just threw that rule away because, once again, you couldn't think straight because you were under the influence of whatever potion you cooked up."

"I made a mistake. It was a hard day, and I needed something to help me through. I'm sorry, and I promise it won't happen again."

"You're sorry? Do you understand that if what happened today gets out, I'm going to have to return to the Abyss? Worse, we could have been killed and heading there right now. You promised me you were going to get help, and you lasted a week."

"What do you want from me? I told you I was sorry, and it won't happen again," Shalik snapped.

"I know it won't because I can't trust you to manage the club or our business like we used to, and I think it's time I just shut everything down."

Shalik's eyes widened. "But you love Valaria. It was your dream ever since you came to Fusion City."

"Yeah, well, I guess that dream died along with everyone else last year."

Before Shalik could answer, there was a knock at the door. Selena already knew who it was and pushed to her feet. Everyone else would have had to wait for her to come down to the side entrance that led directly to her apartment or to the front of the club, but not Raesean.

She yanked the door open to a well-dressed Raesean standing there with every hair in place and his hands in his pockets. She wondered if anything ever ruffled him.

His gaze traveled down her legs and back up to her eyes, face remaining carefully blank.

"Is this a bad time?" he asked.

She rolled her eyes at him, then turned and walked back to the living room. She thought she heard a hiss of breath but didn't bother to investigate. Whatever his problem was, it was his problem. All she wanted to know was if she needed to pack.

The door slammed shut behind her. Raesean's footfalls went from loud on the tiles in the entryway to cushioned on the carpet in the living room.

He unbuttoned his jacket and took a seat on one of the sofa's matching armchairs. Selena plopped down on the sofa where she was before while Raesean settled himself on his "throne."

"What happened?" he demanded.

"They hired us to do a party for a teenage dryad. Turns out that teenage dryads look a lot like rogue demons trying to kill me for the death and torture of their cousin."

Raesean blinked at her flippant response before taking a deep breath. "I thought you could read beings better than this?"

"I can," Selena said, struggling not to look at Shalik.

"So how did Lima trick you into believing they were dryads?"

"It was my fault," Shalik butted in. "I took the interview via phone, even though I knew it was a risk."

"I see," Raesean said, but Selena could have sworn she smelled traces of sulfur from the fire he produced. "Shalik. Can you give me a minute to talk to Selena alone?"

Shalik looked to Selena, and she jerked her chin. He stood without a word and moved to the kitchen. Only when she heard him puttering about with the kettle and mugs did she turn back to Raesean.

"What's wrong," Selena whispered. "Were we seen?"

"No, and I took care of everything else so that the only things that remained in that room were piles of ash."

Selena breathed a sigh of relief. "Then why does your face look like the world is ending?"

He moved so he was sitting next to her on the sofa.

"Abaddon contacted me tonight."

Selena tried to jump to her feet, but Raesean grabbed her arm to keep her still. "He wants you to return to the Abyss because you're in danger up here."

"What?" she snapped.

"The rogue demons who came topside aren't just looking to get away from your father. They are working with Belial. He leads the biggest demon army in the Abyss, and Alden, his nephew, was like a son to him. He wants revenge, but more importantly, he wants to overthrow your father. You are the ticket to him getting what he wants."

"He's not blood. They would never let him rule," Selena pointed out.

"Yes, but that's not stopping him from trying."

Selena wiped away a drop of water that fell from her hair onto her thigh while she turned Raesean's words over. When she looked back at him, his gaze was following the motion. She cleared her throat, and he looked up into her eyes, shifting so that there was more space between them.

She fought the twinge of disappointment she felt. "What does that mean for me? Should I just lie low until the whole thing blows over?"

"You're not getting it, Selena. Abaddon will not leave you unprotected in Fusion City, where any being can get to you."

Selena's stomach sank because she knew exactly what Raesean was going to say next.

"He sent me to collect you, your friend, and your little dog too."

"There is no way I'm going back to the Abyss. Not after everything I did to get out."

Raesean stretched out his legs, one ankle over the other. He itched to run his hands over the legs and curves that were currently pacing in front of him. Rather than give in to temptation, he casually linked them over his stomach.

"I thought you might say that, but need I remind you, you made a deal with your father to return to the Abyss for three days, and he is calling in his payment."

Selena stopped her pacing and smirked. "And how is he going to enforce his deal? Is he going to leave all those souls and demons unsupervised and come get me?"

"Nothing as drastic as that." Raesean got to his feet. Reaching inside his jacket, he pulled out the small silver disk. There were symbols carved on one side using the old language of the demons. On the other was a mixture of his and Abaddon's blood. It was a talisman. An old demon token that allows the demon you made a deal with to force you to complete the deal you made.

Selena took a step back. "You wouldn't dare."

"You know I would." The corner of his lips tugged up as he watched a myriad of emotions play across her face. From anger and outrage to confidence and deviousness—she was planning something.

"I hate to burst your bubble, but when I made the deal with Abaddon, we never shook on it, considering we only spoke via the mirror, and every demon knows a deal is void if you don't shake on it. So that talisman will not work on me."

Raesean flicked the silver two-inch-wide disk like a coin up in the air and caught it on its way down. "You must really be scrounging for excuses if you think that's going to work on me."

"I don't know what you mean."

A nervous flick of her tongue to her bottom lip and Raesean knew he had her.

"You and I both know you don't need to shake the king of the Abyss's hand in order to make a deal. That's only for regular demons like myself. So the deal you made with him is very much in effect. Now quit stalling, go pack what you need for a week or two, and let's go."

"Two weeks? I only made a deal for three days," she screeched.

"That was before you tried to back out of your deal. He's charging you interest."

"What's going on?" Shalik asked, abandoning his pretense of trying to make tea. Selena didn't bother to answer, just stomped to her room, slamming the door behind her. She let out a thin scream that gave Raesean a thrill of pleasure.

He shifted his gaze over to the next problem he had to deal with. Shalik was like Selena's brother, and she would never go to the Abyss and leave him behind as fodder for the demons looking to hurt her. But at this moment, Shalik was a liability.

Raesean took in his disheveled appearance, uncombed hair, and red-rimmed eyes. He was addicted to something, and Raesean would bet his club it was something Shalik cooked up for himself. The man was too talented to depend on an outside person to give him what he needed.

He walked around the sofa, erasing the distance between Shalik and himself.

"I couldn't begin to understand what you're going through, and I know you're probably still grieving, but what you're doing to yourself is not helping either of you. Your carelessness almost cost both of you your lives."

"I already apologized to Selena, and this is none of your business."

"This is very much my business. She is the daughter of the king of the Abyss, and I am currently second in command. So while she is in Fusion City, everything involving her is my business, and that includes you."

He took a step closer, crowding the potion master even more. "So you're going to go pack a bag for two weeks, leaving behind every single thing you used to make that potion you're addicted to."

Shalik scoffed. "You can't force both of us down to the Underworld with you. You don't have that power."

Raesean waved the talisman in front of Shalik's face. "Do you know what this is?"

"No, but I don't see what that has to do with us going to the Underworld."

"Let me enlighten you, potion master. When you make a deal with a demon, you tether yourself to that demon until both sides fulfill their end of the bargain. If either party doesn't, then the other can force them to their will for a time. Abaddon has temporarily transferred his ability to enforce his will with the use of this little talisman."

"Okay, but Selena made the deal. You may be able to force her, but not me."

"Are you sure about that? When the deal was made, did Abaddon specifically say Selena needed to come to the Abyss, or did he just use the general term *you*? Not to mention, you also wanted something from Abaddon even though she was the one who made the deal. But if you don't believe me, then don't pack those bags. I'd be happy to force you down to the Underworld, and it would be painful."

Shalik huffed and flounced off, much like Selena did.

"Oh, and Shalik," Raesean called after him. "Be prepared to dry out in the Underworld because I will not have you put her life in jeopardy again. If you so much as look at an ingredient for a potion, I'll have the demons down there torture that addiction out of you."

Chapter 6

The SUV winded its way through the city streets like a menacing shadow. Everything on it was blacked out, from the rims to the windows.

Selena had never seen Henry driving it before. He usually only drove Raesean around in a town car. She supposed Raesean opted to use the SUV as it could carry all three of them plus the overnight bags they'd packed and her dog, Cerberus.

As though he knew she was thinking about him, the dog let out a loud whine from his cage in the back. Shalik shushed him, reaching into the cage to calm him down. Cerberus hated riding in cars.

Selena looked at the immaculately dressed demon sitting next to her. He'd forgone his usual white suit in order to match his black-on-black car.

"Tell me why we couldn't open a portal using a mirror and step right into Abaddon's home?"

Raesean peered at her from the corner of his eye. "You're really asking that question after what you did to those demons back at the party?"

Selena shifted so that she was looking out of the window instead of at her father's second. "I defended myself. What's wrong with that?"

"Nothing would be wrong with it if it were your usual style," Raesean countered. "But you slicing everyone to ribbons and preparing to rip Lima's soul out of her body to send to your father is not the way you do things. You're more diplomatic than that."

"How would you know?" Selena snapped.

He gripped her chin, forcing her to look at him. "Tell me what's going on. No bullshitting."

Her gaze darted to look at Shalik in the back seat before coming back to him. Her actions were enough for him to release her. He eyed her for a beat before turning away. She supposed she was lucky he didn't push the matter because she wasn't ready to face the changes in her magic, nor did she want to discuss it with Shalik.

The last thing she needed was to add worry to his grieving plate.

"I thought we could only get to the Underworld by portal," Shalik commented, probably hating the mounting silence.

"Upper-level demons usually use portals, but that involves some of our ancient spells, and I thought it would have been more comfortable for both of you this way."

"So we're going to drive all the way to the Abyss?" Shalik's tone was thick with sarcasm.

"No. Only to the gates."

Hours ticked by, and Selena could hear both Shalik's and Cerberus's snores in the back row. The scenery from the window faded from the busy city streets of East End to the dangerous, run-down ones of West End. The contrast between the two was like cupcakes and chili peppers. East End was where all the law-abiding citizens lived, trying to move up the hierarchy and make lots of coin. East Enders' sole mission was to make it big and be famous.

West End was mixed with those wanting to live a life of debauchery. The rule in West End was survival by any means necessary, be it robbery or murder. Some West Enders didn't choose this life—they were born into it. Others, especially demons, thrived on it.

There weren't many rules to keep them in check, and they could find the chaos that they thrived on on any street corner if they looked hard enough. Drugs, females, deals to be made, whatever you wanted could be found in West End.

Except for your heart's desire.

That was exclusively Selena's territory. Her magic allowed her to see into your heart and pull out its genuine desire. Shalik was the potion master who could make a potion to temporarily grant you your wish.

They drove past Raesean's club, where she'd first met Mini and Shalik. Back then, their money-making enterprise comprised of her using her magic to mesmerize their marks so that they could dream their hearts' desires. Then Mini and Shalik would relieve the marks of all their valuables.

Selena's face lit up with a soft smile.

"Remembering the good old days?" Raesean's words broke into her thoughts, and she turned in her seat to look at him.

"Sometimes I wonder if things would have been better if I'd stayed in West End. If Mini would still be alive and..."

"No," Raesean said, cutting her off. "Alden would have found out your secret sooner. If not him, then someone else, and who knows what they would have done. I'm sorry you lost Minerva, but you escaped with your life, and I'm glad for it."

Selena fell silent once again, turning back to watch the streets get narrower. Buildings became fewer and far between. Everything got darker as they drove closer to their destination. Raesean wasn't lying when he said they were going to the gates of the Abyss.

There was an entrance at the very edges of West End, away from where any random person could stumble upon. If you weren't a demon and wanted to reach the gates to the Underworld, you had to survive crossing West End and still figure out how to make it reveal itself.

It was another hour before the SUV came to a halt, and Henry turned around to face them with a nod.

"Thank you, Henry. I'll call if I'm coming back this way."

The overhead lights clicked on when Raesean opened the door to step out. Shalik stirred in the back, stretching his arms over his head with a yawn. His head swiveled back and forth, his mouth hanging open at what must have been the most shocking sight of his life.

"Where are we?"

Cerberus let out a sharp bark. He could probably smell the sulfur and river water from here.

"We're at the gates to the Abyss," she responded.

"I don't see any gates. All I see is a wasteland of ash that can double as our grave if Raesean decides to kill us. Are you sure we can trust him?" Shalik opened the gate of Cerberus's cage, petting the wiggling, excited bundle of fur. He knew where they were going. She hadn't realized he'd missed his home.

"Trust me. This is where the gates are. Someone just needs to open them." Selena slipped out of the car, her booted feet crunching on things she didn't want to think about. A wind picked up, blowing some of the ash her way. She quickly pulled up the scarf she was wearing over her nose and mouth.

"Glad to see you remembered how to dress." Raesean looked over the lightweight navy hoodie she wore under her dark leather jacket and thick leggings tucked into her boots.

"I've crossed this more times than you can count. I know how to dress to survive a trip to the Underworld."

He smirked. "I sometimes forget you were a boatman once, carrying the souls of the dead to the Abyss."

"We prefer the term Charon, thank you very much."

Footfalls growing near had Selena turning to face Shalik. Dressed in a similar outfit to hers, he carried both of their backpacks and Cerberus. She took her bag from him with a nod of thanks and slipped her arms through the straps, freeing her two braids from under them. All the while, Raesean took in her every move.

"What?" she demanded as she adjusted the weight on her back.

"When I'd said pack for two weeks, I was expecting a lot more luggage." He slid his hands into his suit pockets. "I didn't think you'd pack like you're in survival mode. You're usually dressed so..."

"Diva-esque," Shalik supplied. The two shared a grin, and Selena rolled her eyes at them.

"Just because I like nice things does not make me a diva."

"And I suppose the giant closet with everything coordinated doesn't make you a diva either?" Shalik bumped her hip with his.

"Whatever," she said, stomping off to the sound of their snickers. "If anyone here is a diva, it's Rae, with his designer suit and styled hair."

"Technically, I'm on the job, so I must look the part," Raesean said.

"Right. I forgot that's all I am to you." For some reason, his words stung. Maybe she should be grateful that's all she was to him. After all, it's never a good idea to get involved with a demon.

The three were silent as Selena walked on, using her magical connection to the Underworld to find the gate. It took another fifteen minutes before she found it.

"This is it," she said. Raesean and Shalik's footsteps crunched closer to her. "Do you want to do the honors, Rae, or shall I?"

Raesean moved up to her side. Slipping a switchblade from out of his pocket, he flicked it open. Selena didn't acknowledge Shalik's deep inhale and waited for Raesean to open the gate.

With considerable skill, he pressed the pointed end of the knife to the tip of his index finger, drawing it downward. Blood welled to the surface, and Raesean laid his bloody finger on the invisible gates while chanting the words "reveal" and "open" in the ancient demonic language.

The vast, tall, rusted iron gates shuddered into view. They comprised thick bars and decorative whorls that sometimes ended in sharp, pointed ends. Part of the gates bulged outward as though something from the other side had made it here and tried to bust its way through. She hoped whatever it was had been caught and returned to wherever it was supposed to be.

Cerberus barked, his body squirming to get down.

"Don't put him down," she warned Shalik. "He'll just take off to go find his siblings, and then it'll take ages to find him again."

"I didn't know he had siblings," Shalik said, holding the struggling bundle closer.

Selena shrugged, not wanting to elaborate on the large number of siblings Cerberus had. "Yeah, he has quite a few of them, but he's the only one that's so spoiled."

The dog huffed as though in disagreement.

Selena turned her attention back to Raesean and the gates. He arched his brow as if to say "ready," and she nodded her head in return. After one last look around at the ash-filled wasteland, they walked toward the gates. They swung open with a groan that sounded like a whispered welcome.

She hadn't been through these gates since she'd come to Fusion City years ago. Now that she was going back, she had to admit that she was a little curious about what lay in wait on the other side.

Raesean and Shalik followed her through the gates, and after a beat, they clanged shut behind them, the barren lands winking out of sight. Shalik gave a little shudder, but she didn't think it was one of excitement.

"Where to now?" he asked.

"To the river. We need to catch a boat."

The ground beneath them was no longer covered in ash with an unidentified crunch but was hard and black like cooled lava years after a volcanic eruption. Cracks ran through the ground in a haphazard pattern, with a fire-red glow coming from them. It was the only light source in the otherwise twilight-lit area.

Selena breathed in deeply, seeking the part of her connected to the Abyss, the part that allowed her to sense souls and carry out her previous job as a Charon. The souls on the river called out to her, begging for her help, and she knew exactly which direction to go in.

"This way," she said, leading the way down a steep path. The trio traveled in silence. The only sounds were their feet hitting the hard-packed earth and Cerberus's occasional excited bark that echoed over the distance.

"How do you know we're going in the right direction?" Shalik asked after they'd taken another steep turn before heading even further downward.

"My magic told me," she replied.

"But... how?"

Selena let out a sigh. It was difficult to explain to a non-magical person how your powers worked, but if this kept Shalik from getting too much into his head about where they were going, she would oblige.

"Everything brought to life in the Abyss has a connection to it. It's dormant until you tug on it. When you do, you can use it to sense other things like it in the Abyss."

"Is it the same for everyone?"

"No. For me, I seek the river. For Rae..."

"I seek the fires of the Underworld," Raesean supplied.

"If you're brought to life here, then there will always be something that connects you, and you'll always find your way back."

"Some just take longer than others," Raesean said with a pointed look at her.

"I would have preferred never to come back," Selena snapped.

"So you say." Raesean eased past her on the path, taking the lead to the river, and she scowled at his retreating back.

A breeze blew in, cooling the sweat that had built up on her neck and face. They were getting closer. Raesean picked up the pace, and Selena matched it, tightening her grip on the straps on her back.

The ground changed from hard rock to rich black sandy soil, stretching all the way to the river Ebon. Boats bobbed at the water's edge, and a thick white fog covered every other part of the river and even some parts of the sandy land.

"We need a boat," Raesean said, heading purposely to the floating vessels. Before she could warn him, a black-hooded figure stepped out of the fog at the water's edge, its black and silver scythe arching down to remove Raesean's head.

Chapter 7

Heat blasted out, slamming into Selena's chest.

She stumbled, dropping to her knees as Raesean covered his entire body in the hottest blue flames. His hands were palm up and open as the scythe inched closer to his neck.

He increased the intensity of the flames, forcing the Charon to jump back. The bony fingers peeking out of the long black sleeves of its robe tightened around the metal staff of the scythe. Its hood was pulled low so that its face was permanently shadowed, but its glowing red eyes tracked every movement Raesean made.

"What's the meaning of this, boatman?" Raesean demanded. His hands closed into fists, just before sliding them into his surprisingly intact pockets. Nothing on him caught fire, even though he'd covered his entire body in flames. It was more like an impenetrable halo.

"You sort to steal a boat, and that is not allowed," the Charon responded. His voice sounded old as time itself. A weathered tone that suggested it had been around long before sunlight hit the earth. It was the voice of death itself, and it sent chills down Selena's spine.

"You would deny Abaddon's right-hand man?" Raesean took a step toward the Charon, not even phased that this being could send him back to Amaryllis to be reborn again.

"Just like you, demon, we, the carriers of souls, have our own rules. No one but a Charon can steer a boat to the Abyss." His gaze finally left Raesean and landed on Selena, kneeling in the sand. She climbed to her feet, adjusting the bag on her back.

"I am a Charon, and I'm here for a boat," she said. Then recited the words known only to the carriers of souls. "It can be sweet."

"Or bitter," the Charon responded.

"Broken."

"Or whole."

"Among the living."

"Or the dead," he finished. "It's been a long time since you've navigated these waters, Selena."

"Not long enough if you ask me."

The Charon tilted his head, his glowing red eyes staring at her. "You've been blessed with an ability that every one of us would love to have, yet you squander it."

"Taking the souls of the dead was never my thing; I'd much rather use my magic to grant people's desires. In fact, I'd happily hand over my abilities to you if I could only sit peacefully in my club instead of being dragged a long way down to the Underworld."

The Charon stared at her, but she didn't care. She just wanted to grab a boat and get to Abyss as soon as possible. Everyone always had an opinion on her magic and what she should do with it, but no one ever considered what she wanted.

He eyed her a bit longer, then pointed to a boat anchored some distance away.

"Remember the rules of the river," he warned, fading back into the fog.

"What the hell was that?" Shalik asked from his seat in the sand. Raesean's display of power had knocked him on his ass, and he'd yet to stand.

"Let's go before any of the others show up." Her boots left footprints in the sand as she crossed it to the boat.

"How many are there?" Raesean asked, winking out the flames that had surrounded him.

"I don't know, but... this Charon is one of the milder ones."

"Do they all look the same?" Shalik asked, finally catching up to them.

"More or less," she responded. Selena waded into the shallow edges of the water and threw her bag into the boat. "All aboard."

Shalik handed over Cerberus, and Selena gave him a scratch behind the ears before gently placing him in the boat. The bundle of fur sniffed around before sprawling out at the stern of the skiff. Shalik climbed in next, unceremoniously dropping his bag and finding a seat in one of the rowing positions. Raesean climbed in and took the other.

With a last look at the shore, Selena climbed into the boat. She unhooked the wooden pole attached to the starboard of the skiff and used it to push the boat completely into the water.

"You're good at that," Raesean noted, observing how she efficiently guided the boat into the water, replaced the pole, and then used the tiller to steer the boat down the river.

"It was my job, remember?" Her brown eyes met his blue ones, and he gave her a small smirk. "Anyway, gentlemen. There are rules to being on the river. First, keep your hands inside the boat. Do. Not. I repeat, DO NOT stick your hand in the water."

"Why?" Shalik asked.

Selena gave him the hard look the question deserved. "You are alive. This river wants dead souls to take. Do the math. Also, if you see or hear anything strange, close your eyes, block your ears, and tell me immediately. Sometimes, the river can play tricks on you. Whatever it shows you is not real, so ignore it."

"I didn't realize crossing the Ebon was so hazardous," Raesean said, looking around at the black water surrounding them.

"When was the last time you crossed the river?"

"Point taken."

"Which is why I don't understand why we couldn't go via a mirror portal. This is such a waste of time." Selena huffed.

"You know why, Lena. You may not want to face it, but your magic hasn't been the same since that night, and I wasn't about to risk your life over a portal."

"What?" Shalik demanded. "What's going on with your magic?"

Selena shot Raesean a glare that would have surely killed him if she had used magic. She shifted the tiller, angling it in the direction they needed to go before answering Shalik's questions.

"I'm not sure if it's my magic or the pendant, but since I used it in the ritual with Alden, the pendant has turned blood red. I think it's now connected to blood magic, which is harder to control. When I use the pendant, it's as though the magic is controlling me and not the other way around."

"That's bad, Selena. How could you not tell me this?" Shalik rubbed a hand over the knee of his jeans.

"You had your own problems, and I didn't want to add to them." She looked away from him, knowing that that wasn't the complete truth, but it was all she was willing to give.

Her gaze locked on Raesean's, and he arched a brow at her.

Did he see the truth? The real reason she'd kept this new facet of her magic to herself.

It was a heady feeling, the magic. Darker, more powerful, more destructive, and it demanded its due. She'd grown up around enough demons to know that flirting with dark magic—blood magic—will only send you down a rabbit hole, but some days it calls to her, and it was a struggle to ignore.

"The water is turning bright," Raesean said, bringing her out of her thoughts.

She looked over the edge and noted the normally dark blue liquid had streaks of lighter blue, yellow, and green. The further they moved forward, the wider the streaks got.

"We are passing through the area of lost souls. Remember the rules. Hands in the boat, and if you see anything that looks strange, tell me."

The water in the river continued to change color. The greens, blues, and yellows spread and blended until they were wide streaks in the dark water. It glowed bioluminescent and mesmerizing as the boat continued to channel through it.

"What's causing the water to change color?" Shalik asked.

She could practically see him itching to dip his hand in. Cerberus growled at him, and he linked his fingers together in front of him.

"Souls," Selena said, patting the dog at her feet. He wiggled in appreciation.

"Souls of the lost," Raesean murmured. "Rumor is that sometimes souls don't make it across the river to the Abyss, but I didn't know they ended up here in the river."

"The souls here wind up in the water for a myriad of reasons. They see a loved one in the water and opt to be with them there.

They'd rather stay in eternal purgatory than face the punishment waiting for them in the Underworld." Selena shrugged.

"Or some of them get sucked into the water because they wouldn't keep their bloody hands in the boat," Selena snapped, stopping Shalik from reaching over the side of the boat.

"I wasn't going to stick my hand in the water." He rolled his eyes at her. "I was just pointing. There's a face in the water."

Selena and Raesean looked over the side of the boat. There was indeed a face in the water. A woman with big almond-shaped eyes and a gentle smile. Her face was the light yellow of water, and her hair swirled in blue waves. She floated next to the boat, keeping pace with them as they neared the port of the Abyss.

"She's just saying hello," Selena said. "Don't engage with her, otherwise you might attract something else."

"The music she's playing is soothing."

"What music?" Icy tendrils of fear slithered over her body, and she looked around frantically. The red glow of the Abyss port was still some distance away.

"It's like I can feel it over my skin." Shalik leaned further over the boat. His eyes glazed white as he reached a hand out to touch the woman in the water. "She's speaking to me, but I can't understand what she's saying."

"Rae. Grab him," Selena commanded. The demon grabbed the back of Shalik's hoodie and shoved him into the small space at the bottom of the skiff. He sat on the potion master to keep him from getting back up.

Selena's fingers tightened on the tiller, wishing the damn boat would move faster. Whatever Shalik was hearing meant the river was targeting him.

"Lena."

"What?" she snapped, shifting her gaze back to Raesean. The flickering of his eyes between the familiar blue to the white film similar to what was now covering Shalik's had the pit of her stomach churning more than the water they were on.

She swore.

"I think I can hear the music he's talking about." Raesean's eyes were staying white longer and longer.

"Guys, I just need you to stay with me." She gauged the distance they still needed to go. "Just think, in a short while, we'll be on Abaddon's level, and he'll be trying to get me to eat those nasty vegetables he grows. Maybe you guys could help me set fire to them."

Raesean chuckled. "He'd be pissed to hear you say such a thing about his garden."

"You still with me, Rae?"

"Barely and not for long."

"We're almost there," Selena lied.

As though to prove what a liar she was, the once smooth water swirled, making small waves. Selena bit her lip as she watched the blues, greens, yellows, and black moving together to become rainbow waves that started lapping at the sides of the boat.

"That doesn't look good," Raesean said, eyes glued to the water getting higher and higher at the sides of the boat.

Cerberus barked at whatever entity he was seeing and she wasn't. The water rose, taking on the shapes of various people, and Selena knew it was some of the lost souls in the water.

If they spoke, she didn't hear them, but she knew their outstretched hands weren't inviting the occupants of her little skiff for a relaxing swim.

Raesean lifted his hand, then lowered it, shaking his head as he fought the effects of what he was seeing.

Selena looked in the distance, gauging how far they still had to go. They would never make it to shore if she didn't do something soon. She had to use her magic with the very pendant that was slowly taking her over. If she didn't, the river would take both Shalik and Raesean from her. She just hoped she kept her control and didn't lose herself completely to the magic.

Magic.

Her magic.

She dropped the tight reins she kept on it, and it flowed through her as though it'd been waiting for her to reach for it. Selena let it fill her, flooding the blood-red pendant around her neck. The pendant fell apart as though crushed. Its tiny particles floated around the boat like someone had thrown a handful of glitter in the air.

They hung like stars in the darkness, forming a barrier between the boat and the water figures reaching for Raesean and Shalik. The water churned, the figures splashing water to wash away the dangling mirror particles.

"I guess you don't like that," Selena muttered. She removed one hand from the tiller to reach into the side pocket of her backpack. Pulling out the mirror she stored there, she threw it up in the air, using her magic to guide it to the center of the boat.

She chanted, repeating the words for the spell to transfer souls to the mirror over and over again. The lost screamed as she pushed her magic out, shouting the words louder. One by one, her magic sucked them into the surface of the small disk, wavering like mercury as it pulled in the souls. She could hear them screaming, pounding on the other side of the mirror, trying to escape.

It was a heady feeling being in control of someone's afterlife. Knowing you could dictate what happened to someone once they'd left this world. No one else she knew had this power, and she relished it. It made her feel stronger, like she could control everyone's fate with a push of her magic. Just like she could control the fate of those in the river.

She could suck every soul from the water into her mirror and gain more power to do with as she wished. Maybe she should. She could have an army of the dead to haunt, to possess, to rule. Then she wouldn't be at the mercy of fate; she'd be able to protect her friends, her family, from anything that came for them.

Sucking in all the souls from the river would give her all the power she needed. Yes, this was a great idea. She was going to do just that.

Chapter 8

Raesean blinked away the mental fog he'd been in. The magnetic music and the warm voices faded, to be replaced by thousands of screams and a barking dog.

He looked around. They were still in the boat, and the water was churning, bashing against the side of the vessel. Before he'd gotten lost in the fog, it had been yellow, blue, and green. Now, a bright white light covered it as though someone was shining a spotlight on it. Tendrils of that light were coming up from the water, arching over the boat and up to the glowing circle above. Its reflective surface rippled, and Raesean knew exactly what it was.

He looked over at Selena. Her usual copper skin was glowing like a beacon. One hand directed her magic to pull the souls from the river into the mirror above. Her lips were moving, but no words were coming out. Her eyes were silver like the mirror, unseeing yet focused on the tendrils of light popping out of the water.

"Selena," he shouted. He reached a hand to touch her, but the light sliced his hand like a blade through butter.

"Shit," he cursed, yanking a handkerchief from his pocket to wrap his hand. "Selena," he tried again.

Cerberus continued to bark at her again and again, making his own attempt to wake her up from this trance she was in. The boat rocked, forcing him to grip the sides. He stole a look over his shoulder and saw that the port was fast approaching.

Selena's other hand was wrapped tight around the till as though, even under the control of her magic, she wanted to get them to the shore. But with the white light around her, he couldn't remove her hand from the till to slow the boat. If he couldn't get her to wake up, they were going to crash right into the port, and he wasn't sure if they would survive.

The boat bounced again as the water lowered the closer they got to shore. He gave the till another look. She was holding the end. Maybe he could break off the part she was holding and use the rest to guide the boat.

The skiff bounced over a rocky surface, signaling they were out of time. Grabbing Cerberus, Raesean tucked him down next to Shalik on the floor, then used one hand to call his magic. He tossed a fireball at the tiller, burning through the old wood like a gas-soaked rag. The part Selena was holding fell into her lap, and she frowned as though the pain she felt was bringing her back to reality.

"Wake up, Selena," he tried again. The boat hit another rocky surface, this time pitching upward. They were airborne and coming in for a crash landing. Raesean didn't have time to do anything but force his hand through the pain of Selena's magic, grab her arm, and yank her to the floor.

Gravity sucked the out-of-control boat down hard, and it landed on the banks of the river with a hard crack. Every part of Raesean jostled, but he kept a tight grip on the damn dog and Selena's arm.

The boat bounced once, twice, before slamming to a complete halt. Sand and rocks flew everywhere, raining down on the shaky habitants of the impromptu roller coaster. Someone let out a groan, and Cerberus trembled in his arm.

He looked down at the thumping on his thigh to see a dark honey hand pounding at him.

"Shit." He laid the dog down and climbed off the chest of the potion master, who wasted no time sucking down some much-needed air.

"Did... we... survive?" Shalik gasped, scrubbing a hand over his chest.

"By a hair," Raesean muttered. He brushed some of the splintered wood from the skiff off of his suit, then checked on Selena.

Her eyes were closed. One leg hung off the port side, and her hand still gripped the broken till. There was a lump on her forehead that he was sure she got when he pulled her to the floor.

He shook the arm that was still tight in his grip.

"Are you back with me, Lena?"

She moaned, eyelids fluttering before they eased open.

"What happened?" she cried, dropping the till to the cracked floor of the boat. Raesean gently pulled, helping her to sit up. He leaned in, inspecting the bump on her forehead.

"Doesn't look too bad," he muttered. He wanted to run his hand over every inch of her just to make sure there weren't any more bruises or broken bones. Instead, he pulled away while she prodded the bump with a wince.

"Don't touch it," he warned. "You'll only make it worse."

He straightened and looked around the area. Other Charons were ferrying more souls in without so much as a glance their way. It was as if the crash landing of a skiff on the shore was an everyday occurrence.

Raesean stepped off the wreck, feet crunching on the rocky sand. He noted that some of the souls were already lined up following a guide of the Underworld down a path leading deeper into the other levels. He fought back a shudder.

He'd always hated the guides. They were creepy beings. Soulless—brought back only to take the souls where they needed to go. Their skin was made up of patches from different dead demons sewn together quilt-style until they were covered in a demon-skin cape. They had no eyes or lids, just empty sockets that eerily reminded him of the deepest pits in the Abyss.

Cerberus let out a sharp bark, bringing Raesean's attention back to the boat. Selena and Shalik were gingerly climbing out of the ruined skiff onto the ground.

"What happened after the music started playing?" Shalik asked, reaching to grab the backpacks that miraculously stayed in the boat. He handed Selena hers first, then grabbed his.

"The lost tried to get you both into the water where I'm sure you would have drowned, and your souls would be eternally trapped in that river."

"That much I remember." Raesean slid his hands into his pockets. "But what happened with your magic, Selena? When the fog of voices had cleared, you were sitting there brighter than a lighthouse, and the souls of the lost were screaming in terror. What did you do to them?"

Selena brushed debris from her backpack before slinging it over her back. "I took them."

His brow lowered as he turned her words over in his head. "You took the souls from the river? I thought that once you entered the water, there was no way to get out."

"It seems I found a way." Selena picked up a wiggling Cerberus, running a hand down the dog's back. Raesean suspected it was more to comfort herself than the dog.

"Did you know you could do that?"

"I didn't, but I had to try something so you both didn't end up in the water."

"Yeah, but we almost ended up there anyway because something went wrong with your power, and you started sucking up more and more souls, like a kid with candy at Halloween."

"What do you want me to say, Rae?" Her eyes turned silver with her anger. "That I lost control of my magic. That the power I felt sucking each and every soul into that mirror felt amazing, and right at this very moment, I'm fighting not to head back out onto that water and suck every soul from it."

"You can do that?"

"I don't know, but I was certainly willing to try."

Raesean let out a sigh. Maybe he should have let her open a portal there. At least if she'd lost control, he would have been conscious to stop her from sucking the life out of everyone around. He wondered, if he hadn't awakened in time, what would have happened. Would she have turned on him and Shalik next?

"Where's the mirror now?" he asked.

She huffed out a breath, handing off the dog to a worried-looking Shalik. Then she called on her power.

"Selena," he warned, wrapping his hand around her arm to stop her.

"It's okay." She laid her hand on his. "I'm not going to use the pendant. I'm just calling it back to me, along with the mirror with the souls."

He looked at her for a heartbeat, nodded his head, and then released her. He didn't move too far, remaining close in case things went wrong.

With a push of her magic, the air filled with sparkles. Tiny pieces of mirror floated through the twilight to her from off of the sea where they'd dropped when the trio had crashed the boat. The sparkles merged to reform the pendent previously attached to the necklace around her neck. The red-tinted glass glittered at him, mocking his concern for her.

In the distance, a larger disk came hurtling through the air toward her. Selena held up her hand, palm up, and the mirror he'd spied above the boat when he'd first woken up lowered into her hand. She closed her fingers around the circular mirror, and he could hear the faint voices of the souls in it screaming.

"Can you... can you set them free?"

She ran a finger over the now solid surface. "I don't know."

"Even if you break it?" Shalik asked. His eyes were wide, and he looked a little spooked.

"I truly don't know," Selena said. "But I don't want to risk breaking the mirror and extinguishing the souls. When I get to Abaddon, I'll ask him how he removed Alden's soul from the mirror."

Raesean nodded, then held out his hand for the mirror. "So you don't get tempted."

She hesitated, then dropped the reflective circle into his palm. He slipped it into the inner pocket of his jacket before he turned to look at the souls marching uphill to be judged and placed in their appropriate levels.

"We have to follow the guide until we get to Abaddon's level," Selena said, moving to stand beside him.

"I know. I was just getting a lay of the land."

"How long until we get to Abaddon's level?" Shalik asked, standing on his other side.

"About an hour if there're no problems."

"Are you expecting problems?" Selena asked, once again taking the lead.

"With you? Always," Raesean muttered.

Chapter 9

Selena led the trio up the rocky path behind the line of souls heading to their various levels. None of them would know where they were going until judged and sentenced. Some would go to purgatory, also known as the Fields of Asphodel, where they would wait to meet up with loved ones and toil in the lands until their soul released any guilt they had. Only then could they go to the Lucien level to await the angels, who would swoop in to take them to Elysium.

Only the blackest of souls would go to the pit, where demons would eternally torture them. There was no escaping the pit, no matter what you did. Most souls ended up in one of the two levels: the Fields of Asphodel or the pit, but on rare occasions, an amazing soul would go directly to the Lucien level to meet the angels who would take them to Elysium. There, they would spend the rest of eternity with everything their soul desired.

The smell of sulfur got stronger the further up they climbed. The souls filing up the hill looked at them, but none interacted. It was as though they could sense how unstable Selena was at that moment. Her magic had calmed, but not by much. It felt like it remained right under her skin, ready to be unleashed at a moment's notice.

She'd never had problems controlling it before, but now that she'd used the pendant in a death ritual, it was like it had come alive and wanted more. Shalik moved closer to her side, and she reached a hand out to scratch under Cerberus's chin.

"You want to talk about it?" Shalik asked. His gaze met hers expectantly.

"Not really," she responded. There was a beat of silence.

"I'm sorry," he whispered.

She frowned. "For what? It's not your fault my pendant is now linked with dark magic and is demanding power."

"For being a shit friend these last few months. For not seeing that you had your own struggles."

"After all the shit I've put you through these last few years, I guess it was my turn."

He gave her a small smile. "I suppose you're right, but I'm still sorry I put you in danger, and now you might have to give up everything you had to work for. I know the club, Valaria, was your dream."

"Not everything." She bumped her shoulder against his. "If we stick together, we should be okay. Maybe we could start over somewhere else."

"You planning to leave Fusion City?" Raesean interjected. His voice was hard, as though something she'd said had angered him.

"If you must know, Mr. Nosy, I haven't decided yet." She looked at him over her shoulder. He was walking with his hands in the pockets of his suit pants as though taking a leisurely stroll through the park. Meanwhile, her breath was shrinking the more she hiked up the hill. If they didn't reach the Gates of Judgment soon, then it was going to be nonexistent.

"I wasn't being nosy," Raesean said, interrupting her thoughts. "I was simply curious as you were speaking clear enough for me to hear."

"Fine," she conceded.

"Don't forget. You made two deals last year, and you haven't fulfilled either until today."

Selena stopped in her tracks and spun to face Raesean. "If I remember correctly, you decided you wanted nothing to do with me and whatever is going on between my father and me. So it sounds to me that the deal not being met is a *you* problem."

"You're right. I'll get right on that as soon as we return to the city."

"Not a chance in the..." Her words trailed off as she realized what she was going to say.

Raesean's grin was wide, and his blue eyes lit up. "In the Abyss? Then I guess I have a huge chance, as that's exactly where we are."

Selena heard Shalik snickering behind her, and she turned, punching him in the shoulder before she stomped off.

"I'll let you know the time and place, Lena," Raesean called after her.

She flipped him the finger over her shoulder, and he laughed.

The rest of the journey to the Gates of Judgment was in silence as Selena opted to conserve her energy in case she had to punch Raesean in the face.

She had to admit, her anger at him calmed the magic under her skin. Maybe kicking his ass was the key to resolving her magic issue. She would love to try out that theory.

The nerve of the demon. After he'd been so quick to cut off all ties with her, now, he wanted to demand the date she owed him. She didn't want to admit it to herself, but last year, when everything had been happening, she'd considered breaking her no-demon rule for him, but then he'd done a one-eighty on her.

Nope, he had a rude awakening coming if he thought she was going back down that road with him.

The ground beneath them leveled out, turning less rocky and more earthy. A wide clearing stretched out in front of them, smelling like a mix of sulfur and newly tilled earth. The number of feet that crossed it had trampled it flat. Even so, little shoots of green fought to poke through. The line of souls they'd been following stopped to look at the tall gray gates in front of them.

"What's happening?" Shalik asked. His eyes were wide as he took in what stood before the gates.

"We've reached the Gates of Judgment," Raesean answered for her.

Four beings stood in front of the gates, waiting for the souls to gather. A demon would take the condemned souls to the pit to face their punishment. A being mixed with human magic and other things Selena couldn't identify took the other souls to purgatory. The third being was something no one knew. It was more of a shadow shaped like a person who dispensed judgment.

The last being was one she wanted to avoid at all costs. She'd forgotten the angel had been assigned to take the rare souls to the upper levels and sometimes to Elysium.

"Let's go," Selena whispered. She didn't want to spook the souls waiting, and she really didn't want to get the attention of the four beings standing by the gate.

She inched right, shifting away from the souls heading to the gate. The path that would take them to Abaddon's level loomed closer, and they remained undetected like Selena wanted. They were a couple of feet away from the path when Cerberus let out a loud bark.

Selena froze. The swoop of wings extinguished any hope that no one had heard her dog. She took a step back when the angel landed two feet away from her.

"Haven't seen you in a while, Selena."

"Hello, Reuel."

She looked into the citrine eyes of the angel standing before her. White wings spread wide, the tips colored a pale gold so that it looked like they were glowing, even in the dim light. The tall male was a fine handmade specimen of the higher power, and his attitude depicted his knowledge of it as he swaggered forward.

He held up a small brown wedge between his thumb and index finger, and when Selena realized what it was, she gritted her teeth hard enough to almost crack them.

The angel transferred the wedge from his fingers to his palm, stepping past her to feed the treat to Cerberus.

Betrayed for dog treats. The rat bastard.

She gave Cerberus the evil eye. No doubt he smelled it the moment the angel held it up, but the dog ignored her, munching happily on his own version of the thirty pieces of silver.

"Don't look at him like that, Lena. I sensed you the moment you landed on the shore. I was just waiting for you to show up."

Shalik cleared his throat, bringing Reuel's attention to the potion master currently holding her dog.

"Hello," Reuel said with a smile. Not one to understand personal space, he remained two hand lengths away from Shalik, who was staring into the angel's face in awe.

"Hi. I'm Shalik," he said.

"Reuel."

"Now that you two've met, we need to be going," Selena muttered.

Reuel's smile wilted around the edges, and he stepped away from Shalik to get closer to her. "What's your hurry? I thought we could hang out a bit like old times. I haven't seen you in ages."

"That's because I haven't been down here in a while, Reuel, and I don't plan on staying here longer than I have to."

"If you're only here for a short time, then it's all the more reason for us to catch up." He stepped even closer, invading as much of her space as he could. "Things haven't been the same since you left."

Selena felt a twinge of guilt. When she'd taken the chance to hide in Fusion City, she hadn't given a second thought to everyone she was leaving behind. Reuel being one of them. There'd been a spark of something between them, but the chance at freedom had been a golden opportunity, and she never looked back.

"Reuel, I'm..."

He placed a hand under her chin, lifting her face to better look into her eyes. "I've missed you."

"I don't think she's missed you, angel." Selena stiffened at the sound of Raesean's voice. A spark of light traveled across Reuel's eyes, and he dropped his hands, turning to look at the demon.

Not one to hide in the shadows, Raesean stepped forward. His signature antagonizing smirk in place, and his hands in his pockets.

"Is that what you've been up to, Selena? Slumming it with the demons? I would have thought you had better taste than that."

Selena bristled at his comment. "Who I associate with is none of your concern, Reuel."

The angel ignored her, taking a step closer to the demon. "I would say it was a pleasure to see you again, Raesean, but we both know that angels can't lie."

"No, they only tell half-truths and let you jump to conclusions," Raesean pointed out. "Give me a good liar any day. At least I know where I stand with them."

The angel's wings fluttered, a sure sign he was angry. "I see you're still down here as Abaddon's lackey."

"Actually, I was in Fusion City with Selena, as Abaddon's right-hand demon. It's part of my job to keep my eye on *every inch* of his daughter to make sure the next ruler of the Underworld is safe."

"That's enough," Selena snapped. "If you guys want to measure dicks, then do it when I'm not around."

"Why would I need to do that? I already know mine is bigger," Raesean said, waving a hand dismissively.

Lightning sparked over the angel's tightening fists.

"Go ahead," Raesean taunted. "The demons' pit would welcome another fallen angel. They haven't had one in a long time."

"One day, the Abyss will be destroyed, and you'll burn in your own fire, Raesean."

"Until that day, then."

The angel scoffed and turned back to Selena. "Come see me when you've gotten rid of the riff-raff."

Without waiting for her response, he shot into the sky, white wings gleaming in the dim light of the Underworld.

"Must you piss off everyone you know?" Selena demanded, hip cocked.

"No," Raesean said, "but with him, I relish it."

He walked past her, heading down the path to take them to Abaddon's level.

Shalik followed behind, muttering under his breath to Cerberus. "I should have brought popcorn."

Selena took a deep breath, letting it out before following the others. If one more thing happened before she reached her father's place, then she was going to lose her shit.

They walked in silence, Raesean in the lead and Selena lagging behind. She wasn't in the mood to keep up with his angry stomps all the way to her father's level, and since his legs were longer than hers, it would have been near impossible to do so anyway.

Shalik fell back until he was side by side with her.

"You okay?" he asked.

"Why wouldn't I be?" she huffed out. "The trip here just keeps getting better and better. I can't wait to see what happens when we get to Abaddon's place."

"Do you think there's going to be trouble?"

She sunk her teeth into her bottom lip, thinking over his question. "I'm not sure. The thing is, Abaddon wants me down here to establish that I'm going to take over the Underworld and also as a deterrent to those demons trying to kill me."

"But..." Shalik prodded.

"I know demons and once they set their sights on something, they go after it until they are dead. Only severe punishment would serve as a deterrent, and there is only so much of that you can dole out."

"So you think things are going to go to shit either way?"

"Pretty much. Or maybe I'm just being negative because I'm tired and grumpy and think this entire trip was a waste of time because somebody was being overly cautious about my magic."

"Selena," Raesean shouted back to her.

She rolled her eyes at the somebody in question. "We could have taken a perfectly good mirror portal to my father's place, but oh no, you insisted on taking the long route."

"Selena," he called again. This time, his tone was harsher.

"What?" she snapped.

"You're going to want to hurry and catch up with me."

She frowned, looking past him to see a group of very large demons lumbering their way.

"Is that what I think it is?" Shalik asked, clutching Cerberus close.

Selena sighed. "Well, it's definitely not the welcoming committee."

Chapter 10

They were huge.

Rumbling up the path, their footfalls shook the ground with every step closer. Selena counted ten of them, and there were probably more hidden behind the front line.

"What do you think they want?" Selena asked Raesean when she reached his side.

"Considering these beasts look like they're from the pit, I'd say someone sent them to either kill you or take you down there."

"How do you know they're from the pit?"

"The size of them, for one thing. Their completely black eyes, for another. There is no light in the pit except for the fire used for torture. So anyone living down there has to adapt in order to survive. The first thing that adapts is the eyes."

"I've never seen demons like this before," Selena observed.

"You wouldn't have," Raesean countered. "Not unless you'd spent time in the pit. Just like they wouldn't know about you because I doubt Abaddon would have taken you down there to watch souls being tortured."

Selena watched the eight-foot giants coming closer, their gaze intent on her.

"If they're here to kill me, I'm going to have to use my magic, Rae."

"No," he demanded. "I don't want a repeat of what happened on the boat. Especially with all those souls we left back at the Gates of Judgment. If we run into complications, you and Shalik run when I tell you to."

He looked over at the potion master to get confirmation that he heard what to do. The trio stood watching the demons approach until they were a few feet away. One of them took another step closer, and Selena concluded he was leading the group.

"Why are you out of the pit?" Raesean demanded.

"Raesean. Second to Abaddon. Greetings," the leader said.

"I care not for your greetings. Only to know why you're out of the pit." Raesean's hand remained loose at his side, his legs apart, ready to attack if he needed to. With his crisp suit and straight spine, everything exuded power.

Here, at this moment, he wasn't the flirtatious demon who showed up in her room in the middle of the night. He was the right hand to the leader of the Abyss, and he wielded that power like a weapon.

Power looks good on him.

The demons before him looked at each other. The lids of their eyes widened so that Selena could see the black Raesean spoke about.

"They sent us to stop anyone from coming up this path," the leader said.

"Who sent you?"

"Our instructions come as they always do, as whispers in the dark."

"Then we will be on our way," Raesean said.

"I'm sorry," the leader said, shaking his head from side to side. "We cannot let you pass."

"Only Abaddon himself can tell me where I cannot go in the Underworld, and since he's expecting us, I suggest you move out of our way."

The giant demons from the pit all shifted on their feet. The leader of the group was practically wringing his hands.

"Like you, we have our orders, wraith. The whispers we hear are said to be from Abaddon himself. If we disobey him, we will not only lose our chance to see the above but we will be punished. My brothers and I will not submit ourselves to the mercy of the angry king of the Underworld. We fear much, and fear is a weapon in his hands."

Raesean lifted his hand, flames enveloping it from fingertip to wrist. "You call me wraith, yet you refuse to obey my command."

Even in the dark color of his eyes, Selena could see the fear in them.

"I do not refuse. I just cannot obey your command unless Abaddon or his proven heirs can counter the command of a whisper."

"How do you know if someone is heir to the Abyss?" Selena cut in. She could tell by the set of Raesean's shoulders that he was ready to lay flames to the demons. Maybe it was the dilemma they were facing or the distress that was coming off of them in waves, but she felt a little sorry for them.

"To prove you are an heir to Abaddon, you must perform magic that is like his or rare and dark magic that can only be found in the Underworld."

Selena tapped Raesean on his shoulder, jerking a thumb over hers to let him know she wanted to talk away from the demons. Raesean backed up a few steps, keeping his eyes on the demons. They stood passively, waiting for him to strike.

She never would have thought it possible to see a nonviolent demon. They were like big teddy bears just following orders. If they were like that, were there other creatures that just did their job because they were forced to?

"Don't even think about showing them your magic, Selena," Raesean commanded before she could even get a word out.

She folded her arms over her chest. "One. You can't tell me when I can and can't use my magic. You work for my father, you aren't him. Two. I wasn't going to suggest using my magic. Whose soul am I going to suck out?"

Raesean smirked. "I have a way you can suck my soul out without the use of your magic, and you can call me Daddy when you do it."

Selena rolled her eyes, but she had to bite back a smile at his innuendo.

"So what did you have in mind?" Raesean asked with an arched brow. He probably knew the direction her mind had taken.

"I was thinking of using Cerberus."

Raesean frowned. "Don't get me wrong, your dog has a certain appeal to him, but I don't think his cuteness is going to win over the demons from the pit. They are bred to punish and guard the entrances of the pit from any souls that try to leave."

"That may be, Rae, but they're still living creatures. They seek freedom from the life they were born into, just like the rest of us."

Raesean finally shifted his gaze from the demons to hers. He held it for a moment as though he was thinking over the words she'd spoken. Then he snuffed out the flames on his hand, sliding it into his pocket.

"Alright. This time, we will do it your way, but if you fail, then I'm going to move them my way."

Selena nodded, hoping that what she was about to do worked and the nice demons didn't get flambéed.

Nice demons. Was there such a thing?

Turning to Shalik, who had silently stuck to their sides since the demons walked up, she took Cerberus from him, scratching the top of the dog's head as she moved toward the demons.

"You guys might want to take a few steps back," she called over her shoulder to Raesean and Shalik.

"Not a chance," Raesean said, falling in step with her.

"Suit yourself," she responded. "Now, Cerberus, we're back in the Underworld, and I need you to do some defending. We need to go see Daddy Abaddon."

The dog whined, then let out a sharp bark.

"This is not a negotiation. I need you to defend me, and you can't do that like this."

More barks followed, and the dog turned his head away as though to say he wasn't going to do it.

Selena sighed. "Fine, if you defend, then I promise extra treats for a month."

He looked at her, then turned away again.

"Fine, two months, but that's my final offer because I know you'll be sneaking treats every chance you get from Daddy Abaddon."

The dog wagged his tail, then wiggled to be let down. Selena took that as a sign that he'd accepted the terms of the deal.

Putting him on the ground, she took a step back, watching as he shook and then stretched with an enormous yawn.

All the demons were watching the little ball of fluff with amazement on their faces.

"Lena," Raesean warned.

"Shh," she hissed. "Cerberus. Defend."

With a series of barks, he wiggled and stretched some more. His cute brown fur fell off in large clumps, his limbs and body lengthened, getting wider and bigger by the second. Cerberus's usually brown skin split, and sleek black fur spilled out against his body. He continued to grow, forcing Selena to take a few more steps back.

His paws widened, getting bigger while his body grew. The nails in them protruded out until they looked like claws, sinking into the dark earth. His normally fluffy tail extended until it looked like a whip behind him, ready to incapacitate anything with one swing.

Selena heard Raesean and Shalik let out a few curse words as the dog continued to increase in size. Its neck enlarged, and a head popped out on either side, swelling until they were the same size as the original. Their ears pointed to the sky, looking like horns on either side of their heads.

The razor-sharp teeth they sported overlapped each other, and Cerberus bared them proudly, growling at the demons in front of him. When he was back to his full size, magical bracelets clamped around each of his legs, and an orange flame rolled down each of his heads, then down his back.

Selena walked under the guard to the Underworld's gates until she was in front of him.

"Good boy," she whispered. He barked, and the vibrations rocked her on her feet. She had to brace against his leg to stay upright. He leaned a head down, and she rubbed her tiny hand under its massive chin. "I'm just going to talk to the nice demons over there, and then you can change back. Okay?"

His tail thumped, shaking the ground. She hoped Shalik and Raesean were out of its reach back there. "Now sit."

His behind dropped with a thump, and the ground shook like an earthquake.

"Selena," Shalik shrieked.

"Just hang on a minute," she called back. She walked over to the demons, who stood frozen as they took in the enormous three-headed dog before them.

"Is this enough to prove that I'm Abaddon's heir? After all, only one from Abaddon's bloodline can command the guardians of the gates and have them transform."

Actually, that wasn't really accurate. Cerberus and his siblings will only transform if they want to, but they are required to listen to Abaddon's bloodline. Sometimes, though, Cerberus conveniently forgets that.

"Yes, my future queen. You may pass." The demon bowed his head, and the others followed. Selena's magic shifted inside her.

It was as though it was reveling in the acknowledgment and fear the demons gave her.

"Thank you," Selena said, hurrying around Cerberus to get back to Raesean before her magic came out to play.

"Let's go," she said to the males standing far enough away to avoid Cerberus's wagging tail. She patted the dog on his flank. "Treat time."

The dog wasted no time. He stood in a rush, reversing the process to shrink down to his smaller stature. It was always a marvel to watch him transform. She wondered how he could shrink and grow so easily and where all the extras went, but he probably had shapeshifting magic that allowed him to change forms.

Once Cerberus was back to his travel size, Selena took out two treats from her bag pocket and fed him. She scooped up the mutt, who happily crunched on his treats, while Raesean and Shalik approached.

"Why is it that every time I'm in a situation with you, some facet of magic comes out that tries to give me a heart attack?" Raesean's gaze jumped between her and the dog in her arms. If she didn't know better, she would have thought he was a little freaked out.

Naw, it couldn't be that Raesean was afraid of the dogs of the Underworld.

Cerberus barked as though trying to unnerve the usually unfazed demon, and his pale skin went a shade lighter.

"You're always full of surprises, Selena." He gave the mutt a pointed look, then led the way past the demons who were all kneeling, waiting for her to walk past.

Shalik took Cerberus from her arms and rubbed his fingers on the top of his head.

"If I'd known I would have gotten so much excitement in the Underworld, I would have encouraged you to take a trip down here sooner," he said with a wink at Selena. He followed Raesean past the demons.

Selena adjusted her pack, muttering under her breath, "You haven't seen anything yet."

She trailed behind, pushing down her magic, which was preening in the reverence the demons were showing her. She hoped once she got to Abaddon's level, she could get it back under control and not suck up the soul of some unsuspecting being.

That might just force her to extend her trip down here like her father wanted.

Chapter 11

Fifteen minutes, and then she would be back in the place she once called home.

As Selena neared the huge white and gold pillars marking the exordium of Abaddon's level, giant moths flapped their wings in her stomach, causing her fingers to tighten on the straps of her backpack. Nothing much had changed since she last stepped foot on this level.

The group walked past the gold-marbled pillars. The story was they were brought down from Elysium. Abaddon kept them as a reminder of home. Selena looked to the right of the paved walkway they ambled across. Her father's garden was thriving with the disgusting vegetables he insisted were good for her. There'd been many fights when she was little whenever he insisted she eat them.

To the left was the lake she'd spent hours on, lying in the boat and looking up at the faux sunlight shining down. She'd only learned that the sunlight was fake after her first trip to Fusion City.

"How is there sunlight down here?" Shalik whispered, interrupting her trip down memory lane.

"Abaddon had a witch create the illusion so that his level would look like the human realm," Selena responded.

Raesean watched from the corner of his eye but didn't comment on her response. The full truth was that the witch who created the illusion was her mother, who left in the first few years of her childhood, or so she was told. She didn't tell Shalik that because she didn't want to talk about her mother. Especially when she was this close to seeing her father after she, too, had left without a word.

"Why is it so quiet?" Shalik went on.

Selena shrugged. "It's always like this outside. Inside's livelier."

They approached the wide front door of the sprawling manor with its high ceilings, brown and cream brick walls, and manicured hedges that lined the edges of the property.

Before they could knock, the door flew open, and out stepped the king of the Underworld.

Selena took in the tall stature of her father, his broad shoulders covered in a designer suit that highlighted the bronze undertones of his sandy skin. His short, curly hair was close to his scalp, and as usual, the angel had tucked his black wings away.

At first glance, no one would think the being sent from Elysium was anything but a friendly angel. They would be dead wrong. Abaddon had a thirst for punishment and torture and would wield his power to pull out a being's desires or fears to repeatedly shatter a soul.

The angel, now banned from Elysium, tugged on the cuffs of his shirt and looked them over, and a wide smile lit up his face.

"It took you guys long enough to get here. Did you take a detour to another level first?" Abaddon stood before her, his gaze traveling over her from head to toe. "You look as though you've been through the wringer."

"That's what happens when you take the long way here and some giant demons from the pit try to stop you from passing." Selena's voice was flat as she looked at her father. She still wasn't sure how she felt about being back, but she would not show any emotion that could be considered a weakness.

She had been trained time and time again on the many trips to the various levels of the Underworld. If you were going to rule the Abyss, then no demon could see any chink in your armor. Emotional or otherwise.

"Demons," Abaddon said. He looked over at Raesean. "From the pit? What were they doing out of the pit?"

"Apparently, they were told by you through whispers to stop anyone trying to enter your level."

"I see."

Raesean and Abaddon's gaze locked in silent communication until Abaddon looked back at her. "Since you had such an adventurous time getting here, why don't you head to your room, and later, we can discuss... things."

Selena arched a brow. "Things?"

"Yes, we'll discuss it later." He turned, heading back into the house, leaving Selena with her mouth hanging open. "Raesean, let's chat in my office."

Raesean looked at her and silently followed his boss up the front steps and into the manor, leaving Selena, Shalik, and Cerberus gaping outside.

"I guess your father's not big on introductions," Shalik murmured, running a hand over Cerberus's head.

"No, he's usually very curious about the people in my life. I think something's up, and he's distracted."

"Ms. Selena. Abaddon asked that I lead you to your rooms." The soft voice had Selena looking at the doorway. The girl looked young. Well, younger than Selena by a few years. She was also pretty, with big brown eyes and skin the color of a new foal. Her face looked familiar, but Selena couldn't place where she knew the girl from.

"Have we met before?" Selena asked, climbing the three stairs until she was on the same level as the girl in the doorway.

"Oh no, ma'am. I've only been here a year, and I've never seen you visit before." The girl bobbed into a shallow curtsy.

Selena took a longer look at the girl. Something about her was setting off Selena's curiosity, and not in a good way. More like alarm bells. Then it hit her. "You're not a Sacrodaemon."

A quick smirk crossed the girl's face, then it was gone in a blink. If Selena didn't know better, she would have thought she'd imagined it.

"No, madam," she whispered.

"What's your name?"

"Evanora," she replied.

"Okay, Evanora. Lead the way."

The girl turned and sauntered down the dark-wood-floor hallway. Selena stole a glance at Shalik's face before following down the hallway. His frown was deep and filled with curiosity, but he was smart enough not to ask questions in front of a stranger.

Evanora led them through the maze of cream hallways trimmed with white wood. Paintings, framed photos, mirrors, and slate doors to rooms broke up the never-ending walkway.

After a few twists and turns, the girl halted in front of a door. Turning the handle, she threw it open with a flourish. "This would be Shalik's room."

The room was masculine, with its dark blue and black tones. An enormous bed sat against the far wall, covered in pillows and matching sheets. The nightstand was the same shade of wood as the bed and the dresser on the opposite wall.

Selena's eyes roved over the room, then turned back to the girl.

"And where is my room?"

"It's right next door," she said, taking a few steps over to the next door, a taunting smile on her face.

Before she could open it, Selena grabbed her shoulders and shoved her face-first into the door. "Nice try, witch, but this isn't my room. Who the fuck are you, and what do you want?"

The smirk she'd tried to hide earlier returned in full force. "How'd you know this wasn't your room?"

"I grew up here. Just because I wasn't here for a few years doesn't mean I don't know every corner and dust mote of this house. Not to mention Abaddon doesn't have witches as servants in his home."

Evanora scoffed before jamming an elbow into Selena's side, forcing the air out of her lungs. Shalik yanked Selena out of arm's reach of the girl.

"I thought I would have at least gotten you settled before you realized something was amiss, but you seem to have a very suspicious nature." Evanora brushed imaginary lint from her white shirt and black pants. "Don't worry. I'm not here to hurt you. Quite the opposite, really. I wanted to get a peek at who you were."

"Somehow, I doubt it was just for curiosity's sake. So I'll ask again, what do you want?" Selena called on her magic, ready to use one of the many mirrors in the hall to end the girl in front of her if needed.

"It was part curiosity but also to get a lay of the land, so to speak." She looked around as though she was seeing everything for the first time. "I guess I've seen all I need to."

She sauntered closer to one of the mirrors that decorated the hallway, laid one hand on the mirror, and then waved the other in front of her body. The black pants and white shirt wavered, then disappeared, leaving her in a fitted body suit that hugged her body like a second skin.

"You're a mirror witch," Selena spat.

"Ding, ding, ding. Tell her what she's won, Steve." Evanora giggled, amused at her own antics. "It was nice chatting, and I can't wait to see you again when you're in a friendlier mood."

With another wave, she disappeared just like the clothes she had worn before. Selena took the three steps to where the girl had been standing. She laid a hand on the mirror, using her powers to search for any residual magic that the girl might have left behind.

There was something faint on the mirror. A spell similar to what she would normally use to open a portal to the Underworld, a demonic spell. Selena frowned. Few witches knew how to use demon spells. They would have to have been taught by a demon, and witches often found demon magic beneath them.

"What are you doing?" Raesean's voice had Selena and Shalik jumping back to face the hallway they'd walked down.

"Make some noise when you're sneaking up on people, damn it." Selena pressed a hand to her chest.

"I'll be sure to get a bell just for you. Now, what are you doing with that mirror, and why are your eyes glowing with power?"

"I'm looking for a mirror witch who's running around claiming to be a maid." Selena took a breath, releasing the draw on her magic, calming the power, increasing its demand to be used.

"If you're attempting to be funny, you've missed the mark." Raesean took a step closer with his hands in the pockets of his slightly wrinkled suit. The trip here had really done a number on it.

"I never miss the mark when I'm joking, but unfortunately, this time, I'm not." Selena went on to explain what had happened with the maid they met.

"How did you know she wasn't a demon?" Raesean asked.

Selena shrugged. "I don't know, I felt it. Plus, something about her was a little off. I just couldn't put my finger on it at the time."

"Have you always had the ability to sense demons?"

"No. As you recall, the first time we met, I didn't know you were a demon. But after the incident with Alden, I started feeling them everywhere."

"I see." There was a look in his eyes that Selena couldn't quite decipher, and after the trip here, she didn't want to. She was ready to head to bed.

"I think we should head to our rooms," Shalik said. He was still searching the hallway as though Evanora might make another appearance.

"I'm already at my room," Raesean said, jerking his chin at the door that Evanora claimed was Shalik's room.

Selena cursed. "So she'd known exactly what she'd been doing. She wanted me to know this was your room."

"Do you think she was making a threat?" Raesean asked.

"Maybe. Or perhaps she was just batshit crazy. Either way, I would remove any mirrors in this hall and in your room," Selena suggested.

"I'll do that." He leaned a shoulder on the doorframe, then gave Shalik a look. Shalik rolled his eyes, then walked a little way down the hallway, out of hearing range.

"How are you feeling?" Raesean asked Selena.

"I'm fine," she said with a yawn.

He nodded. "I gave Abaddon the mirror with the souls. He said he would extract them, then have them judged and placed on their appropriate level."

"That's good, at least." She scrubbed her booted toe on the carpet. "If I never say this again, thanks for, you know, helping on the boat."

"I was only returning the favor."

"Yeah, well, thanks anyway."

"Are you still struggling with your magic?"

"Funny thing. Whenever I'm annoyed with you, the press of the magic under my skin recedes. Maybe beating you up is the cure for my problem."

"You're on a roll with these horrible jokes today."

"Like I said, I never miss the mark with my jokes," she said with a smile.

He pushed off the doorframe. "Go to bed, Lena. I'll see you at dinner."

She nodded, then headed down the hallway.

"Be careful, Lena," Raesean called after her.

"You too, Rae, and don't forget to remove the mirrors. There's another mirror witch running around, and she seems to have her own agenda. If you recall, the last time that happened, we almost ended up with a one-way ticket to the Abyss."

Chapter 12

Dinner would be a test of his patience and his will to remain Abaddon's second in command.

Not for the first time, Raesean took in the pale yellow dining room with the lightly stained, eight-seater wooden table. It was a lovely room, and he'd had many wonderful dinners here before. The food was always delicious. The problem was the golden boy angel drooling all over Selena on the other side of the room.

He was holding her hand and saying something that made her smile. Raesean wanted to rip the goody-two-shoes' head off. Then he could smile. He hated the fact that Reuel knew Selena, and he detested that the elitist had a better chance of getting with her than he did. Especially as he'd hastily botched whatever they'd started last year.

To be fair, she was the daughter of the king of the Underworld, and the two of them had been feuding. The last thing he wanted was to get in the middle of them. What he wanted to get in the middle of, though, was her thighs as he slowly wrung every drop of pleasure from her. Abyss.

The vicious creature drove him to distraction.

He shook himself, stepped out of the shadows of the doorway and further into the room. As though on cue, the angel turned and sneered at him. Raesean smirked at him.

"I thought this was an invitation-only dinner," Reuel said, stepping in front of Selena as though to protect her. Raesean wondered how much the angel would want to be with her if he knew the witch could slaughter a pack of demons with her pocket mirror.

Such a vicious creature, he mused.

He ignored the preening angel in his hideous gray slacks, white shirt, and hidden wings. Instead, his gaze roved over the delightful witch before him, dressed in a red romper that made her dark skin seem like it was glowing. She'd tamed her mass of curls so that one side was sleek, and the tight coils fell over the other shoulder.

She'd put on makeup so her eyes looked smoky and alluring, even with one brow arched at him in amusement.

"You look lovely this evening, Lena. Your outfit reminds me of the first night we met in my club." As he was prone to do around her, he slid his hands in his pockets.

Selena smiled at the memory. "Ahh. My early days of picking marks in your club."

"You could always return to picking up marks. I won't say no to a boost in business." Helpless not to, he reached out and took her hand. Lifting it to his lips, he placed a gentle kiss on the back of it.

"Tell me he's joking, Selena." The angel's voice grated, ruining the moment, and Raesean took a step back from the pair.

"Joking about what?" Selena asked Reuel.

"That you became a common thief while you were among the humans."

She folded her arms over her chest. "So what if I was? Two of my best friends were thieves right along with me. We did what we had to do to survive."

"Aren't you worried about your immortal soul?"

Selena let out a bitter laugh. "I'm the daughter of the king of the Underworld. Elysium won't even allow the lower creatures to enter their shining gates, so I don't think I stand a chance."

Quick paws on the resin floor had everyone turning to the doorway. Cerberus came through, and Selena scooped up the cute bundle of fur. Raesean took another step away, and Selena's eyes zeroed in on him with a grin.

He didn't care if he was being ridiculous. After all, he petted and held the stupid dog frequently. He just had a healthy dose of caution for things that could survive his hellfire magic and eat him in one bite.

There are several ways he didn't want to die and being eaten by Cerberus was definitely on his top ten list.

A moment later, Shalik entered the dining room, dressed in black slacks and a matching jacket with a pale lilac T-shirt underneath. His gaze took in everyone in the room, and Raesean was pleased to see the mischievous glint in the potion master's eyes that he hadn't seen in over a year. He still had dark circles under his eyes though, and his skin wasn't back to his usual honey tone.

Selena moved to his side with a grin of her own. "Glad to see you made it in time."

Shalik huffed. "You purposely left me so that I would have to wander the halls, only to tease me mercifully when you found me."

She laughed. "Would I do that?"

"Yes," he muttered. "Thankfully, Cerberus here knew the way and led me."

The dog in question wiggled hard enough that Selena had to put him down or drop him. He quickly made his way over to Raesean and climbed up his leg. Raesean had to fight every nerve in his body not to shake the mutt off. As if he knew what he was doing, the bundle of fur grinned up at him.

"What's the matter, Rae? Aren't you going to pick him up?"

He looked between the woman and the dog, realizing they both had the same sense of humor. Not to be bested, he bent down and picked up the wiggling mutt, running his hands down the dog's back the way he knew he liked.

The dog trembled, much like his master did when Raesean had his hands on her. He shifted his gaze to her, and she tilted her head at him, accepting his countermove to her challenge.

"Finally. The gang's all here."

Abaddon's voice broke the moment between them, and everyone turned to the king of the Underworld, sauntering in, dressed in a black suit and a red shirt the same color as his daughter's romper.

Raesean found it amusing that he'd chosen to do that. With all of his fiendish ways to punish evil souls, the man had one glaring soft spot, and it was her. Something the demons trying to overthrow him were quickly beginning to understand.

"Let's eat, shall we?" Abaddon took his place at the head of the table while Selena was on his left and Raesean on his right.

The angel sat on the other side of her, and Raesean wanted to set his wings on fire. He probably knew that based on the smug look on his face. Shalik took the chair next to him. The amused look on his face brightened as he looked between Raesean and the angel. Cerberus, sensing that food and treats were probably coming soon, scampered off to the corner to wait for his bowls to be filled.

"Please bring the food in," Abaddon asked Chaim, the leader of the Sacrodaemon servants in the manor. Raesean had been so focused on the angel that he hadn't seen the Sacrodaemon enter the room.

The male bobbed his head in acknowledgment, then quickly shuffled out, returning with more Sacrodaemons carrying trays of food ranging from crisp greens and succulent chicken to steamed veggies and grilled fish.

Once they'd positioned the food on the table, Abaddon signaled to everyone to dig in. The table was silent for a moment while everyone added what they wanted on their plates.

Selena wrinkled her nose at the vegetables that the angel passed to her, and Raesean snorted.

"What's got my usually stoic right hand so amused?" Abaddon demanded, taking the vegetable tray from Selena and scooping some of the colorful entities onto her plate.

She rolled her eyes at her father and went back to piling her plate with more rice and fish. Raesean would bet his entire club that the vegetables would remain on that plate for the remainder of the night, knowing her aversion to them.

"Rae?" Abaddon said, bringing his attention back to the question the ruler of the Underworld had asked him.

"I was just amused with your daughter's aversion to vegetables."

Selena sent him a death glare while Shalik tried to cover his laugh with a cough.

"Aversion is an understatement," Abaddon muttered. "Those damn things would cause the largest of mutinies in this house. I've punished souls that confessed their sins faster than I could get her to eat those damn things."

Raesean hid his own grin behind his glass of wine while he took a sip.

Selena rolled her eyes at her father. "Maybe if you'd make them taste better, I would eat them. Did you have to make them so disgusting?"

"See what I mean?" Abaddon cut into his meat aggressively. "I specifically created food that could grow in the darkness and nourish you, and you refuse to eat them."

"Excuse me," Shalik cut in, "but you don't really mean that vegetables originated in the Abyss?"

"Of course they did. Though when I created them, it was for the younger demons down here. I didn't think that my daughter would come along centuries later and refuse to eat them."

Shalik looked to Selena, and she mouthed, "Told you."

"I suppose you haven't eaten a single vegetable since you left here."

"That one there forced them upon me," she said with a scoff, waving her fork in Shalik's direction. "He would blend them up in some concoction and wouldn't tell me they were in there until after I drank it."

"Really?" Abaddon turned his full attention to Shalik, and Raesean snuck one of the offending vegetables off Selena's plate.

"How'd you manage that?" Abaddon asked Shalik. "I tried it when she was younger, and she spat the drink right back in my face. Do you know how many suits she ruined?"

"I have a knack for mixing potions, so I can make most things taste pleasant."

"That's a handy talent," Abaddon mused, chewing a bit of his food. "You'll have to mix up some of those for her while you're here because I don't think I'll get her to eat any without a full-on riot."

"As long as Shalik sticks to only mixing vegetables for Selena." Raesean's tone was flat, brooking no room for argument.

The entire table went silent. Two faces filled with curiosity, another with shame, and the last with the fiery temper he loved to challenge.

"Who in the Underworld do you think you are?" Selena demanded.

"It's okay, Selena. Raesean and I have an agreement, and I think he's right. It's better I take a break until I'm more myself."

Raesean had to give it to the potion master. If his threatening to have him tortured was an agreement, then they most definitely do.

"What am I missing here?" Abaddon asked.

"Well, sir," Shalik started. "After I lost someone important to me, I went off the rails a little, and I got addicted to my own potions."

"You must be very talented to use your own magic on yourself."

"But also weak of will," Reuel pointed out.

And here I thought I ruined the mood.

"So anyone seeking to escape their grief is weak-willed?" Selena asked.

Raesean could practically see the storm gathering in Selena as she prepared to let the angel have it.

Shalik was right; he should have brought popcorn.

Instead, he stole another vegetable from Selena's plate.

"Lena," Abaddon whispered. "Leave it be. He's from Elysium. They have their beliefs, and until they've experienced what it's like down here, then nothing you say will change their minds."

Selena turned back to her food, taking a bite and chewing slowly, using that moment to get herself back under control and not fillet the angel. The clueless male just looked at her, wondering where he'd gone wrong.

"Now, Shalik," Abaddon said, steering the conversation onto lighter ground. "Tell me what it was like living on the surface with my daughter."

For the rest of the evening, Shalik regaled the table with the antics he, Selena, and Mini would get up to. Some of them hilarious, others making the angel take another look at Selena.

Look all you want, Raesean thought. *But she's not the innocent angel you thought her to be.*

The evening wound down, and Abaddon stood. "This was a delightful evening. Now Selena, if you've finished your vegetables, let's go to my office. We have a few things to discuss."

Abaddon and Selena looked down at her plate and noted it was completely clean. Raesean wasn't sure who was more shocked, the father or the daughter.

Then the king of the Underworld looked at him with an arched brow so similar to his daughter, and Raesean innocently took a sip of his wine. Abaddon headed for the door, Selena on his heels.

The last thing Raesean heard before Abaddon left the room was an amused muttered, "Interesting."

Chapter 13

Selena followed her father into his office, dropping onto the loveseat in the corner. She kicked her heels off and tucked her feet under her. She scanned the room, taking in the ancient desk she would play under when she was little and her father was working.

Antique books were on the shelves against the wall and piled on the floor. Abaddon would often use them to teach her to read and write demon from them. She was probably speaking the language before she spoke English.

Cerberus came in with a sharp bark and made a beeline for his doggy bed in the corner. Now that they were back in the Abyss, he would have free rein of the place. The huge smile on his face told Selena that he was delighted to be running free.

"This setting looks familiar." He picked up a decanter and poured three shots of whiskey into a short glass. "Drink?"

Selena shook her head no.

Abaddon took a sip of his drink and then leaned against his desk, looking her over. "You look just like your mother. Beautiful."

"Thanks."

"I've heard all the fun stories from your friend Shalik, and Raesean has been keeping me updated the last year or so."

"Of course he has," Selena muttered.

"But," Abaddon went on as though she hadn't spoken. "I want to hear it from you. What was your life like in Fusion City?"

Selena picked at the hem of her romper. "It was good. Despite the difficult beginnings, I was happy. I got to mix with all sorts of people, good and bad. But…"

"But," Abaddon prompted.

"The last year, things haven't been as good. I lost a few people, and to be honest, I'm not sure if I want to stay there. It doesn't feel the same after everything that has happened. I thought that if I could just get everything back on track like before, Shalik and I would be alright."

"But things didn't work out the way you planned."

She shook her head.

"Raesean told me what happened. For what it's worth, I'm sorry about your friend, but at least she's in a good place."

Selena nodded, swallowing back the tears that clogged her throat.

"If you don't want to stay in Fusion City, where will you go?" Abaddon asked.

She shrugged. "I don't know."

Abaddon sighed. "You've been running from who you are for the longest time. Don't you think it's time to return home and take your place at my side?"

Selena's eyes hardened. "Is that what this is about? Me taking your place. Is that why you had Rae keeping tabs on me?"

"Someone had to," he snapped. "After you left without a word, I lost contact with you for years. Then, one day, you just popped up, and I knew if he didn't keep an eye on you, then I might lose you for Abyss knows how long."

Abaddon looked away from her, staring at the one thing that was new in his office.

A mirror.

"What happened to the old one?" Selena asked, trying to break the growing silence.

"I broke the other one after you disappeared and I couldn't find you." He swallowed the rest of his drink, then refilled the glass. "I thought someone might have taken you or you were dead. Imagine my surprise when you showed up looking to make a deal."

Selena chewed her lip. It finally dawned on her how selfish she'd been, abandoning not only the Abyss but her father as well. He'd been worried sick about his only daughter while she'd been building a life, making her own family.

"I'm sorry." She shifted in her seat. "I never meant to leave without telling you. It was just... I saw a chance to live a different life. A life away from all of this and I took it. I knew if you knew where I was, what I wanted, you'd drag me back to the Underworld here."

"I see." He swirled the drink in his hand before taking a sip. "You're so much like your mother. She hated it down here too."

Selena winced. According to her father, her mother had left when she was young and died a few years later. Now she'd done the same thing and left him.

"I didn't hate it down here..." She struggled for the right words. "I don't think I can be what you want me to be. The one to take your place. I don't agree with the way certain beings are locked out of the chance to enter Elysium, and I don't agree that where you're born is where you should remain.

"Good beings come in all shapes and sizes. Not just those who meet Elysium's belief of what's perfect. Pixies, satyr, dryads, even giants. They all deserve to have a place to go when they die. To not have their souls extinguished and never see their loved ones again."

Abaddon sighed. "When they sent me down from Elysium, I had no choice. I'm only allowed to govern by their laws, and I must obey the rules set for me."

"I know," Selena muttered. It was an old argument they'd had before.

"But you, Selena, were born of two worlds. You have celestial power. Did you ever think that you could change the rules?" Abaddon said.

She held her breath, wondering if he was saying what she hoped he was saying.

"You are not bound by the laws Elysium has set. You could change them so all the lesser beings have a place to go after death. The thing is, you need to know them in order to make that change. It's why I was adamant you learn and follow them."

"You can only outsmart your opponent if you know them."

"Glad to see you remember what I taught you."

She smiled. "How do you think I've managed to avoid you for so long?"

Abaddon returned her smile, setting aside his glass. He walked around his desk to take the seat behind it. It was a sign he was getting to the more serious issue that he wanted to discuss with her.

"You need to remain down here as my heir, Selena."

"And here I thought you were seeing things my way." Selena rolled her eyes.

"I see things your way, but you need to see them mine," Abaddon snapped. "If Belial had his way, you and I would be dead, and he'd take my place. Then what would happen to all those beings locked out of the Underworld? Their souls would fade into nothing. They would cease to exist without the chance to have an afterlife like you want."

"But I thought you were immortal?" Selena stood, pacing the short distance between the loveseat and his desk.

"Everything can be killed, Selena, you know this. You just need the right weapon. There have been rumblings of dissatisfaction and descent in the Underworld for the last few years. Belial is planning something. I just don't know what it is."

"I thought the residents down here would only accept someone from your bloodline. If we're both dead, who's going to take over? Plus, I don't think Elysium is going to allow a demon to rule the Underworld. What's stopping them from sending someone else to take your place?"

"Belial sent Lima, his own daughter, to get rid of you, and I'm sure he had something to do with the demons from the pit blocking your way. I don't think they've gotten that far ahead in their plan," Abaddon mused. "Their goal is to get rid of me, take control, then they can run free on the surface."

"Seems like everyone wants a chance to live the life they want freely."

"That may be true, but granting every being their desire would only lead to chaos. Some beings just exist for power and despair, and that is never a desire that should be granted." Abaddon laced his fingers together on the surface of his desk. "But you know that. It's why you blocked those desires when you started your club."

"When Alden tried to bring me down here, he wanted me to be queen and him king. So what's changed since then?"

Abaddon shrugged, the gesture so much like hers. "If I had to guess, he has a replacement, but who, I don't know."

Selena reclaimed her seat, thinking about what her father had told her. "Do you think he'll try to kill me again?"

"If he can, yes. Which is why I insist you stay down here where I can keep an eye on you."

Selena folded her arms over her chest. "I can take care of myself, you know."

"Oh, I don't doubt that. I have had to reassign several souls you yanked screaming out of the river due to you taking care of yourself. A feat that no one in the history of being in the Abyss has ever done. Yet you tell me you're not meant to rule."

"How did you get them out of the mirror?" Selena asked.

He tilted his head at her. "What do you mean? I have power over all dead souls except demons. I can take them out of anything. The difference between you and me is that you don't have to wait for a soul to be dead to control it, and you have your mother's ability to use mirrors, so you can trap them in there."

"You mean I can take them out of the mirror?"

"Yes... You mean to say you never tried to remove them after you trapped them?"

"It's not like I go around ripping out souls to experiment on. When I collected souls as a Charon, the souls would come out of the mirror when I got to the port."

"Would they come out on their own, or would you have to call them out?"

"I would tell them they need to come out and face…"

"So you've been calling them out, and you didn't know?"

Selena stewed over the realization that there was another facet of her power that she didn't know about. Would new abilities develop over time? Was she really the mirror witch who transferred power from one being to another, and she just didn't know?

She shook away the thought. She was the daughter of the king of the Underworld. Her power leaned toward darker things. If it got stronger, it would probably be dark in nature.

"Since the encounter with Alden, my magic's been demanding more… souls. I don't know if it's just my magic or if it's the pendant influencing the magic."

"Let me see the pendant."

Selena took the necklace off and tossed it to her father. He caught it with one hand, looking over the polygon-shaped pendant with its tiny mirrors on each side.

"The glass that made this came from a specific mirror your mother had. It's supposed to amplify your power and any intention you have while using it."

"So when I wanted to rip Alden's soul from his body, that was amplified?"

"It would seem so."

"Then why hasn't it changed its intention? And why is it now tinted red?"

"Tell me exactly what happened."

Selena recounted what happened with Alden the night he tried to drag her down to the Underworld—ending with how she used the mirror particles to complete the symbols in the ritual to open the doorway to send the mirror with Alden's soul to Abaddon.

"I never thanked you for that, by the way. I haven't had the chance to punish a demon soul in a really long time. His fear was so easy to access, it was practically jumping out at me."

Selena arched a brow at her father's pleasure.

He cleared his throat, choosing to return to the topic at hand. "I'm guessing the use of the particles mixed with your blood to complete the ritual somehow corrupted the intentions of the mirror. That's why everything is skewed toward darker demands."

"So what do I do?"

"How about the obvious? Don't use it. Use a regular mirror if you have to, but this one should be retired until you gain a better handle on your evolving magic. In fact..."

He opened the top drawer in his desk and took out a tiny box. Opening it, he dropped the necklace and pendant inside, snapping the lid closed. Grabbing his letter opener, he pricked his finger and then drew a symbol on the side of the box. With a flash, the seam in the box welded shut so that the box was now a smooth-surfaced cube.

"There. Now the temptation is out of your hands." He smiled at her, returning the box to the drawer, shutting it with a snap.

Selena rubbed her neck, feeling the absence of the necklace she had worn for years. "I suppose it's for the best."

"It is. I'll get you a more ordinary replacement for it," he offered.

"Don't worry, I already have several to choose from."

Abaddon shrugged, then sipped his drink. Cerberus let out a loud snore in the corner from his doggy bed, and Selena looked over at him with a smile.

"He seems much happier here, now that he's got the run of the place."

"I don't suppose any being would enjoy spending most of their time in a small space when they're used to having an open field to run in."

"I don't suppose they would," Selena said pointedly.

Abaddon sighed. "I walked right into that one. Look. I never meant for you to feel trapped down here. I wanted you to realize what you could do if you took my place."

"And what's that?"

"Make things different for the lessers. You have the power to help the lesser beings, like the pixies, the satyrs. Even the demons from the pit. I've heard the cries of so many who enter the Underworld, and I'm helpless to do anything for them because I am bound by the rules of Elysium. You are not."

"You think I could make the Underworld different? Better?"

"I know you can, Selena. I raised you to."

Selena swallowed the lump in her throat. If she started crying now, she would turn into a blubbering mess, and her father would only remind her about showing any weakness and how a demon can use it against her.

Instead, she stood, brushing off the imaginary lint from her romper. "I'll think about staying, at least for a while."

"That's all I can ask for and some notice if you decide you're leaving."

Selena let out a dry laugh and glanced over at Cerberus. "And I'll leave the dog with you too."

"Oh please," Abaddon said as he walked around his desk. "You just don't want him to eat any more of your shoes."

"Do you know how much those cost me?" she said in mock horror.

Her father stood in front of her and, without warning, pulled her into his arms. "I'm glad you're home, Lena."

Before she could even return the hug, he stepped away, clearing his throat. "I'll see you for breakfast in the morning."

She bit back a smile, walking past the new mirror on her way to the door. "You should cover that up or remove it."

He frowned. "Why?"

"Didn't Raesean tell you? There's a mirror witch running around. She can enter your office through the mirror. Or even spy on you."

"What was she doing here, and what did she want?"

Selena shrugged. "She said she wanted to get a look at the place."

"Did she give you a name?"

"Yeah. Evanora."

Abaddon stilled, his skin turning ashy.

"What's wrong?" Selena demanded, rushing toward her father.

"Nothing. Nothing. I just remembered something important." He gripped her by the arm, propelling her toward the door. "You must be tired after such a long trip. I'll see you in the morning."

Before Selena could ask any more questions, she was outside his office with the door slammed in her face.

Nothing, my ass.

The name of that witch freaked her father out, and if something worried the king of the Underworld, then it was definitely something.

Something disastrous.

Chapter 14

The stones of the paved path to the lake were smooth under Selena's feet as she walked toward the still water. The "moon" was out, its half-full reflection glittering on the water's surface. She stepped off the path onto the pebble shore, heading for the water's edge.

When she was younger, she would always come here when her thoughts threatened to overwhelm her or the responsibilities of having to take her father's place became too much for her.

She stuck her foot into the water, letting the cool liquid circle up to her ankles, her thoughts on her father.

Who was Evanora, and why did her father react that way at the sound of her name?

"I was hoping I would find you here."

The sound of Reuel's voice interrupted her musings. She turned and watched the angel walking up the path, still dressed in the slacks and shirt he wore to dinner. He'd kept his wings tucked away, and his citrine eyes sparkled in the moonlight.

"I guess you got lucky that I wasn't ready to head to bed."

"Then I should thank Elysium for this divine moment." He stepped close to her, rubbing a hand up and down her arm. The familiar gesture reminded her of all the times he stayed with her while she was out in the boat. "How was the meeting with your father?"

"It was good. Better than I expected."

"Does that mean you'll be staying down here for the foreseeable future?"

"I don't know. I'm thinking about it." She shifted her gaze to look out at the water.

"I've missed you, Selena." Reuel gripped her hands. "And I know your father did too."

"I'm understanding that I did him an injustice when I left without a word."

The angel nodded. "The pull of a life on the surface world is alluring, but life down here is better for you."

Selena narrowed her eyes at the angel. "And why exactly is it better for me, Reuel?"

His grin flashed under the moonlight, and Selena couldn't help but admire how it made his face more handsome.

"For starters, I'm down here, so things are already better."

Selena snorted.

"With you down here, we have the chance to explore," he leaned closer to her ear and whispered, "our mutual interests."

"Oh?" She arched a brow. "And what would those interests be?"

"I'll have to show you." He leaned in, brushing his lips over her cheek. "I wish I could kiss you right now, but there are rules that we angels have to follow."

Selena licked her lips, taking a step away from the angel. "Angels can't fraternize with anyone outside of Elysium without permission."

Reuel shrugged. "I don't make the rules, but I do have to follow them."

"What if you broke them? Would living down here be so bad? You did say it was better for me down here."

"Yes, better for *you*. A place where you don't have to hurt people to survive." He ran a hand through his dark hair, worry marring his brow. "I listened to Shalik's stories, and I'm worried your actions might stain your soul, Selena."

"What does it matter if my soul is stained? Just like every other being who doesn't fit Elysium's rules, they would never welcome me past its gates."

"You don't know that for a fact, Selena. If your soul isn't stained, maybe you can enter."

Selena looked at the angel, at the conviction on his face when he thought she had a chance of entering his world. Her father had been right at dinner. The beings living up there will never see the reality unless they come down and live among the others.

"Then let's hope if I'm judged, I'm not found lacking."

Reuel smiled at her, toying with a loose curl. "Then we agree. You'll stay down here, away from the temptation on the surface."

"Humm. We'll see."

He stepped away from her, not understanding the vague response she'd given him. "I have to go. There are things I need to take care of. As soon as I can, I'll be back, and maybe we can spend some time together."

She nodded.

"Sweet dreams, my sweet Lena."

With a leap, his wings unfurled, and then the angel was soaring into the sky.

Selena watched him go, the gold tips of his wings glittering in the moonlight. She sighed, then headed back down the path.

She made it to the back door of the manor before another voice startled her.

"Reuel is a fool."

"Dammit, Rae." Selena clutched her chest. "What are you doing lurking in the shadows?"

Raesean walked forward, hands in his pockets. He was still in his dinner wear, looking as though he'd stepped off the cover of a fashion magazine. She always wondered if anything ruffled his feathers.

"I wasn't lurking in the shadows. I was simply waiting on the elitist angel to leave."

"Why would you need to do that?"

"Several reasons, the main one being I don't trust one feather on that angel's body."

Selena frowned. "There's something between you two. What is it?"

Raesean looked out at the lake for a moment before facing her again. "Let's just say Reuel is polite to you. To anyone weaker and not in a certain class, he treats them like garbage."

"Are you sure? I know he's stuck in his point of view…"

"Quite sure. I've been at his mercy when I was younger before I became Abaddon's right hand. When that happened, he became a bit more polite, especially when Abaddon was around. The fact that I got my magic and could burn him to a crisp helped him to think twice when dealing with me."

"Rae, I'm…" Selena reached out a hand to him, and he stepped away.

"Anyway. The other reason I came out here was because I wanted to give you this."

Selena let the obviously painful subject drop and instead focused on the item dangling from his fingertips. She sucked in a breath.

"But how?"

"It's not the original," he said, unclasping the chain and moving closer to her. She turned around, allowing him to fasten the necklace around her neck. "I had a replica made. Your father told me you might have to stop wearing the original, and I've never seen you without it, so…"

Selena fingered the replica of the pendant. "It's an exact match. Thank you."

She turned around and realized he was still standing close to her. He reached out, tracing his finger on the chain of the necklace, trailing it over the soft skin of her neck. Then his lips were on hers, and every thought that was in her head eddied out.

His lips were soft but firm, taking what he wanted without hesitation. Raesean's hands circled around her waist, pulling her closer until she was pressed flush against him. She couldn't escape even if she wanted to, and she had no desire to. Instead, she inched her hands up his chest until she got a good grip on the lapels of his jacket to pull him even closer.

A moan slipped past her lips, and it was like a signal to Raesean to deepen the kiss. His tongue dipped past her lips to dance with hers. He let out a groan as though he just tasted the most delectable sweet. Selena's body was on fire, and she wanted to rub every inch against his to ease the heat.

It seemed Raesean had the same idea because his hands traveled down to grip her ass, pulling her against the part of him that was getting harder by the second.

"So sweet," he whispered against her lips.

"Maybe we should go inside," she suggested.

His lips claimed hers again, heating her blood enough that she was ready to strip for him right here in the open.

"Inside," she begged.

He eased away from her, resting his forehead against hers while they both caught their breath.

"Maybe I'm a fool, too, but I think we should wait until your life isn't in such an upheaval before we add another complication to it."

Selena pressed her forehead to his chest, her breath heaving as she fought to get her libido under control. She knew he was right about adding another complication, but her nether regions were not getting the memo.

Raesean lifted her face to his, then brushed a soft kiss on her lips before stepping back. "I'll see you tomorrow, Selena."

She nodded, still a little breathless. She'd already opened the back door when he called to her again.

"Selena." She looked over her shoulder at him. "Reuel will never accept every part of you because he doesn't understand what it's like to fight the dark. To struggle not to unleash the part of you wanting to take control and have everyone bend to your will."

Selena swallowed as she remembered her magic's call to gain power while she was on the boat.

"There is a side of you that leans toward darker things, a viciousness that only comes out when provoked. I accept it just like I do the light in you. The part that wants to fight for the lesser beings in the world."

Selena chewed on her lips as he erased the space between them. His hands found her hair, and he gripped it so her head fell back and her gaze locked with his.

"I'll never be the angel for you, Selena," he whispered against her skin. "I am a demon. So, if there is ever a time when you can't find your way out of the dark, I'll be right by your side helping you burn everything to the ground, and I'll relish every ash that falls at your feet."

***

Raesean lay in the dark, staring at the ceiling, wondering if he was a bigger idiot than the angel.

The kiss he'd shared with Selena was one of the few he'd stolen from her. Even though when his lips were on hers, she melted like an ice cream in the pit, he still needed to know she actually wanted him.

When they'd first met in his club all those years ago, he took one look at her and was smitten. The moment she realized he was a demon, though, she shut him out faster than he could ask her what she wanted to drink.

Then, last year, he'd stolen a chance with her, and he'd realized she wasn't as indifferent to him as he'd thought. Of course, he fucked up that chance by telling her he wanted nothing to do with her. In his defense, he'd thought she was on the opposite side of her father and would eventually usurp him.

After a few conversations with Abaddon, he'd realized his mistake. Selena was racing away from her position as heir, and if given a chance, she would have washed her hands of everything from the Abyss.

His epiphany had come too late. Once on her shit list, it was hard to be removed, and he'd made it when he'd cut ties with her. He was lucky she hadn't sliced him to ribbons in her anger, knowing the vicious creature she could be.

So he looked over her from afar, pining over her in secret like a puppy, making sure no one laid a finger on her. Until the damn satyr had slipped through the cracks, and now here he was once again giving up his chance to be with her because some part of him wanted her to come to him.

He didn't want her to wake up the next morning to claim it was the heat of the moment and it could never happen again. He wanted the chance to take her out, date, and then seduce her. But ever since the moment they met, things have never gone according to plan.

He adjusted the pillow behind his head. Who was he kidding? He would take any scraps she would give him. He'd been doing it for years, looking at her from a distance. Why should he change now?

A groan escaped his lips. He was as stupid as the damn angel. He should have taken her to his bed when she was putty in his hands and shown her, if not with words, with his hands, tongue, and member, exactly how he felt about her.

Maybe he should sneak into her room now and see if the offer was still on the table. He rolled over to climb out of bed, and it was his desire for Selena that probably saved his life.

146

Chapter 15

A sharp sliver of glass embedded itself in the bed where he'd just been lying, leaving a hole in the sheets, glittering in the moonlight coming in from his window.

Raesean stood, flames encasing his hands as he searched for the intruder. He knew it wasn't Selena. Trying to kill him in bed wasn't her style. If she had a problem with you, she confronted you, temper first, then ripped into you verbally and physically if needed.

Another sliver came out of the shadows, but he was ready for it. He threw his flame, and it collided with the shard in mid-air, melting it into a black liquid puddle.

A dark chuckle came out of the shadows, and Raesean turned in that direction, ready to cut down whatever it was.

"Tell me, demon. What were you thinking about so desperately that you couldn't sleep?" the voice taunted.

"Why don't you come out from where you're hiding, and I'll tell you about it."

"I can see why she likes you."

"Is that why you're trying to kill me? Because you have some fatal attraction? If that's the case, then I'd be happy to share," he lied. "Ask anyone in my club. They'll tell you."

There was another high-pitched laugh, then the shadows around the mirror on the back of the closet door thinned, and a petite, slim figure stepped out.

She wore a short red mini-skirt and black top, her feet bare. She'd pinned her curly hair back so it didn't fall in her face, but the curls sprung wildly.

"Who are you?" Raesean demanded. Although he had several ideas about who she was.

"I will not dignify that with an answer," Evanora huffed. She looked around the room, taking in the masculine furnishings and the lack of knickknacks.

"What do you want then?" he asked.

"I thought I would get a closer look at you." She walked over to the bed and threw herself stomach first on it like he wasn't standing there with the fire from the Underworld at his fingertips.

"Your room is a bit impersonal, don't you think?" she asked. She settled herself, propping her hands under her chin, swinging her legs back and forth like a terrible impression of a kid.

"I doubt you came here to give me decorating advice. So what do you want?"

"What does everyone want? Money, power, to be acknowledged and not be a dirty little secret."

"Whose dirty secret are you?" Raesean asked.

She giggled, flipping herself onto her back. "Oh, you smart, smart boy. You already figured it out."

"Figured what out?" Raesean lied.

She pushed up on her elbows, her familiar brown eyes hard and filled with hatred. "Tell your boss I would like a meeting with him. Whenever he's free from torturing all those demons who are rising against him."

"What's stopping me from killing you right here and saving everyone the trouble?"

She climbed off the bed, closing the distance between them. She tiptoed so she was closer to his face. "I can think of two things stopping you from using your fire magic on me."

Evanora twisted into a pirouette and spun back to the mirror she came from. "Don't forget my message for your boss. You wouldn't want me to show up somewhere else and do something destructive."

With those parting words, she stepped back into the mirror, the surface solidifying once she was gone.

Raesean cursed under his breath. This latest development in this war was an absolute shit show.

Selena burrowed closer to the warm body wrapped around her. The rhythmic movement of the hand in her hair helped relax her even more, and she pulled the covers closer.

The hands traveled further down her neck, massaging it and lowering to her back. She moaned in pleasure as the magical hands rubbed parts of her back that had been tense since her trip to the Underworld.

The Abyss.

Her eyes flew open, and she bolted upright, gripping the comforter that was covering her. She twisted to see who was in bed with her. Raesean lay stretched out under her covers, an elbow planted in the pillow, his head braced against his hand.

"What are you doing in bed with me?"

"I was sleeping until you bolted upright." He pulled the cover tighter around him.

Selena could tell he wasn't wearing a shirt under the covers, and the draft on her back reminded her she was naked. Her sleep-fogged brain tried to put together the events of last night. She knew he'd kissed her, and she'd asked him to take her to bed.

As per his habit, he had declined, so she'd come back to her room and taken matters into her own hands. Right?

So how did he end up in her bed?

"Why are you in my bed, Rae?"

The corner of his lips tilted up. "I thought you wanted me in your bed?"

"If I remember correctly, you declined the invitation." She tightened her grip on the sheet wrapped around her chest.

His face turned serious for a heartbeat. "Maybe I changed my mind."

"So, you came up with the brilliant plan to climb into my bed and…"

"Actually, I tried to wake you, but you were comatose, so I took a nap until you woke up. It's not my fault you turned to me in your sleep. By the way, are you always so responsive?"

Selena was glad her skin was a dark tone, otherwise, the blush she felt would have been flaming. "Get out, Raesean."

"Don't be mad. I actually had a good reason to be in your bed."

"I don't want to hear it."

"It's about Evanora."

Selena's entire focus shifted at his words. "Did you see her?"

"She paid me a brief visit last night. I came here after she left my room to keep an eye on you, just in case she detoured here."

"What did she say?"

Raesean hesitated.

"What?" she demanded.

"She wants a meeting with your father."

"Why?"

He scrubbed a hand over his bleach-white hair. It was unusually haphazard. Selena supposed that even perfectly put-together demons get bedhead.

"I need to talk to Abaddon first before I tell you my theory." He pushed back the covers, and she found herself torn between joy and disappointment to see him wearing sweatpants.

"What are you guys hiding from me?" she demanded. She yanked the sheet off the bed, following Raesean to the door.

"I'm not hiding anything."

"But my father is."

His silence was enough to confirm her suspicion.

"Of course he is. Yet he expects me to change things." Selena twisted, then marched for her closet, the sheet trailing behind her. She reached in, grabbing a sweatshirt and some leggings.

"Selena," Raesean whispered.

"Don't worry about it. I'm sure he'll tell me whatever it is when he deems it necessary."

"It may be nothing," Raesean said, and she gave him a hard look, but he went on. "I may be wrong about my suspicions. Let me confirm with him first, and then we'll get to the bottom of things."

"Fine. I guess I'll see you at breakfast." Storming into the bathroom, she slammed the door behind her.

Selena was spitting mad when she entered the dining room, tired of everyone's shit. Her father had dragged her here for her alleged protection, yet he was hiding something important from her. Raesean kept blowing hot and cold on her. Reuel wanted to pick up things where they left off, and there was a mirror witch running around doing whatever she felt like.

She was going to have breakfast and then open an immediate portal out of here.

"You look mad enough to chew glass," Shalik said. He was sitting at the table, piling his plate with scrambled eggs, bacon, and toast. There was a full glass of green liquid that Selena knew contained a type of vegetable.

If he tries to force that on me, he'll end up wearing it.

"What's got your underwear in a twist?"

She shot him a look, taking in his clear eyes, braided blue hair, and chipper disposition. He sounded like himself. The old version of him before Mini died and he got addicted to his own potion. At least there was a plus side to being down here, and if it helped Shalik, she would tolerate her father and Raesean a little bit longer.

"Selena?" His voice brought her out of her thoughts.

"The usual. My father and Raesean." She pulled out the chair next to him and dropped in it, piling her plate with food. "Something's going on, and they are hiding it from me."

"Does it have anything to do with why all these demons are trying to kill you?"

"Probably," she said, crunching into her toast. "Please tell me they brought tea?"

Shalik gestured to the center of the table with his fork, and Selena breathed out a sigh of relief.

"How did you sleep?" she asked him after taking her first merciful sip.

"Great," he said with a grin. "Though I think you might have slept way better than I did, judging from the shirtless demon who walked out of your room this morning."

Selena choked on her second sip, and Shalik patted her back with a wide grin. "Was he as good as all the ladies claim?"

"It wasn't like that. We didn't... nothing happened."

"Sure."

"I'm serious. I woke up, and he was in my bed. He said Evanora paid him a visit last night, and he wanted to make sure she didn't detour to my room."

Shalik swore. "That isn't good."

"I know. He thinks he knows who she is, but he wouldn't tell me until after he had spoken to my father."

"That sounds like things are even worse than we know."

"Now you see why I'm pissed off," she said, waving her cup in front of him.

"What are you going to do?" Shalik took a sip of his green drink, and Selena scrunched up her face in disgust.

"There's nothing I can do. No matter how many threats I make, they won't confess until they're ready. I could hunt down

Evanora and ask her myself, but even if I do, she doesn't look like the type to provide information freely."

Selena's gaze shifted to the doorway when she heard footsteps nearing. The good mood Shalik had put her in threatened to evaporate when she saw her father walk in with Raesean trailing behind.

"Hiding more things from me?" she commented.

Her father let out a sigh while he took his place at the head of the table. Raesean took his place next to her father. They both started piling food onto their plates.

"I don't hide things from you," Abaddon said. "I just don't tell you everything the minute I learn about them. That way, I don't make rash decisions."

Selena rolled her eyes at the implied insult and dug back into her food.

"What's on the agenda for today?" Shalik asked, attempting to break the tension.

"Other than the lake, secrets, and lies, there isn't much else to do down here," Selena muttered.

"How long are you going to go on about this?" Abaddon stabbed into his egg with a fork. "As ruler of the Underworld, I have to make split-second decisions that affect a lot of beings down here, including you. If I think it's something you shouldn't know to protect you from yourself, then so be it. You can be mad at me all you want, but I'll do what I need to do to keep you safe."

"As I told you before, I can protect myself."

"What about the innocents down here?" Abaddon demanded. "Your power is currently unstable. The last thing I want to do is give you shocking news that might trigger that temper of yours, and you go off to hunt down whoever you think needs to be brought to justice."

Selena fell silent at his words. He had a point there. Whenever she was angry, she had a tendency to react before thinking things through. "Fine," she said, crunching down on a slice of crispy bacon. "Have you confirmed your suspicions?"

Abaddon shared a look with Raesean for a beat before Raesean turned his attention to her.

"We've figured out who Belial wants to replace you both with."

"Who? Because the demons down here could only have a leader descending from Elysium."

"Your sister."

Chapter 16

A myriad of emotions danced through Selena at Raesean's words, starting with shock and ending in denial.

"How is that possible?" Her voice was quiet as she continued to process that she had a sibling.

"I think when your mother left us, she was pregnant with Evanora." Abaddon pushed the rest of his food around his plate.

"Then why didn't she return, and why did she leave in the first place?"

"I don't know, Selena. I know she was restless down here, wanted to live above ground, but I couldn't go with her."

Selena fought back her own pang of guilt at how she'd left her father without a word.

"One day, she just packed up her things and disappeared. I sent out scouts, but they couldn't find her, and I'm bound down here for a while longer."

"Then how do we know she's my sister? She could just be another mirror witch claiming to be your daughter."

"The name," he whispered. "It was the second choice we had when we were considering names for you. Eventually, we settled on Selena, but we always said if we had another girl, we would name her Evanora."

Selena thought about her father's expression when she mentioned the name in his office last night.

"You knew who she was when I told you about her last night, and you didn't tell me?"

Her father sighed. "I wasn't sure she was your sister, but the sound of the name triggered thoughts of your mother. After Raesean told me what she said, I'm leaning more toward her being your sister."

"Then there's no actual proof she's your daughter, and Belial could just be making a risky play for your position as king of the Underworld."

"It could be," Raesean said, pointing his fork at her. "But if she's not legitimate, then he'll never have the power he needs to maintain his rule over the demons. It can only come from a being with an Elysium bloodline."

Selena pressed her fingers to her eyes. "What exactly does she want? And why is she working with Belial?"

"She wants a meeting with me," Abaddon said. "As for why she's working with Belial, I don't know."

"When is the meeting?"

"She didn't say while she was dancing around my room. I'm sure she'll let us know soon."

"Or you could tell her when and where for yourself," Selena pointed out. She took a sip of her tea to ease the sudden dryness in her throat.

"How are we going to do that?" Abaddon asked.

"How else do you contact a mirror witch?" Shalik pointed out before draining the contents of his glass. "Through a mirror, of course."

Raesean frowned. "Do you have enough control of your magic to do that?"

"I guess we're going to find out."

The plan was simple. They would set up a large mirror in Abaddon's office, and Selena would scry through the mirror to contact Evanora. If her sister wanted to respond, all she had to do was touch the mirror. It would be like video calling, only via a mirror.

Selena sat in her usual spot in her father's office while Chaim and other Sacrodaemon servants brought in the mirror. She wondered if any of them had known her mother's plans—if they'd helped her escape the Underworld.

"Are you sure you can do this?" Raesean's words jolted her off the suspicious path her mind had taken about the servants. "Are you alright?"

She looked up into his pale blue eyes, and one thought occurred to her. "How did you know she was my sister?"

He frowned. "She looked like you, or didn't you notice that when you saw her in the hallway?"

"No, she doesn't."

"Yes, she does," Shalik chimed in. He was sitting in the corner, away from everyone, with Cerberus in his lap. His brow beaded with sweat as he scratched between Cerberus's ears.

It looked as though he was still fighting off the effects of his addiction, but he seemed to be winning. She didn't ask him about it because she knew him well enough to know he wouldn't want to talk about it in front of the others.

"What do you mean?" she demanded instead.

"She has the same tight curls as you, the same skin tone. But her eyes are a lighter shade of brown than yours."

"And she's less... curvy than you," Raesean chimed in.

"What's that supposed to mean?" Selena demanded, and Shalik snickered.

"What Rae is delicately trying to say is that your ass is bigger than hers."

Raesean slid his hands into his pockets before sending Shalik a hard look that caused the potion master to laugh harder. "It was merely an observation, and stop trying to avoid my question. Are you okay to do this?"

She shook out her hands as though gearing up for a fight. "I think so. Without the original pendant, I don't think I'll have such an onslaught of magic."

Raesean looked her over as though searching for the truth in her words. "Alright then, but if I think you're losing control, I'm going to use any means necessary to bring you back."

Selena nodded, her gaze shifting back to the Sacrodaemon who had set up the mirror on the far side of the office under her father's direction. He stood beside it, looking between Raesean and herself, a small smile on his face.

"Now that we've settled that, let's get on with it, shall we?"

Selena stepped up to the large mirror in its plain frame, calling her magic to the surface as her hands hovered over the glass. Once she was sure there wasn't another spell on the mirror, she opened her hand for Raesean to give her the knife she needed.

With a prick of her finger, she wrote the spell she needed to scry for Evanora through the mirror.

"You've always had a knack for spell work. You probably got that from your mother."

"I don't think so because you taught me everything I know." They shared a smile before Selena sent a pulse of magic into the mirror, along with the spell. "Let's hope that Evanora wasn't lying about her name and her magic."

Selena's magic traveled, following her command, shifting through every reflective object that would show her who she sought—the mirror witch Evanora, who matched her bloodline. If she was near anything reflective, the mirror would show her to Selena.

If she wasn't Selena's sister, a mirror witch, or wasn't someone named Evanora, then she wouldn't be found.

Selena waited as the spell shifted from mirror to glass, to puddles of water, like a card player seeking the perfect hand. Seconds ticked by, then minutes. Yet she sat in front of the mirror, waiting to find the key to Belial's plan.

They were an hour in when the mirror fogged up, and the familiar face of her sister came into focus. Selena now knew who this woman was. Her spell to find her wouldn't have worked otherwise.

Evanora sat propped up by pillows in a red robe, a Cheshire cat smile on her face.

"Aren't you a clever one tracking me down so soon?" she said.

Selena remained silent, still shocked that her mother had had another child and still hadn't returned home or told them anything.

"You requested a meeting with me." Abaddon stepped forward, laying a hand on Selena's shoulder, giving it a quick squeeze. The move jolted her out of her disbelief.

"Why yes, I thought I would introduce myself in person, considering we've never met, but it seems my sister had other plans." Evanora's gaze traveled over the room, taking in every-one who was present. "And look at that, the entire family is gathered together to speak to little old me."

Her voice was mocking, but Selena detected a bit of hurt in the undertone. Was Evanora upset that her father hadn't been in her life?

"Where's your mother?" Abaddon asked.

Selena held her breath as she waited for Evanora to answer.

"Dead. She died a long time ago under questionable circum-stances."

The callous way she dismissed their mother's death jolted through Selena, igniting her rage. The mirror trembled, and her sister smiled. "What do you want, Evanora?"

"My, my. So touchy. As I said before, I would like a meeting with the king of the Underworld. You're welcome to come, Selena. We could play with dolls and do each other's hair and compare notes about our lives these last few years."

"Evanora, you had to have known I didn't know about you. Your mother left us, and I did everything in my power to find her."

"That's unfortunate, considering she was in your own back-yard. Right here on the demon level. What a terrible game of hide and seek you were playing."

Abaddon sucked in a breath, but Selena kept her eyes on the woman wielding her words the same way Selena would her shards of glass.

"Really, Abaddon. You really should keep a closer eye on your demon subjects. They don't like you very much and will lie to you if they think they can get away with it."

Selena reached up and gripped her father's hand on her shoulder, and she watched as Evanora's eyes darkened with anger. "Imagine all those carefully worded reports you received about not being able to find her on the surface when she was right under your nose."

"Who hid her?"

"Everyone did. She was their queen, and they loved her. She spent time with the demons, listening to their plight and trying to find ways to help them instead of punishing them for any minor infraction."

"What do you know about demons? I have ruled the Underworld for thousands of years, and demons only cause destruction if you don't keep them in line."

"Keep them in line, yes. Not enslave them. Most of the demons down here are trapped until the rare chance for them to go to the surface comes up, and even then, they're limited in what they can do."

"The rules about the surface world are not my own. Just like everything else down here, they come from Elysium. You're welcome to challenge them if you'd like."

"Maybe I might."

Abaddon scoffed. "You are young if you think you can take on Elysium."

"That's enough stalling," Selena snapped. "When do you want to meet?"

"Belial and I would like to meet with you in a week. Is that convenient for everyone?"

"Fine," Abaddon agreed. "I'll see you both in a week in my home office."

"That stuffy old place? I was thinking we could have a little dinner party with music and dancing. It would be a nice evening before we negotiate the terms of our ceasefire, as they say."

"You can't be serious?" Selena snorted.

"I'm very serious. Most of the demons down here are sworn to Belial and to me. Which means you're outnumbered. If you so much as try anything, I will open a portal right inside your lovely manor and let every single one in."

"All this for a fancy dinner?"

"Of course not." The curls on her head moved every which way as she shook her head. "I want a father and daughter dance too. I'll keep an eye out for my dinner invitation."

Selena fought the urge to scream at the clearly mad woman in front of her. It wouldn't do well to reach Evanora's level of insanity.

"By the way, Abaddon. The demon level is closed to any-one who's sworn to you. So don't even try to send your spies. You wouldn't want to lose yet another person you care about." Evanora gave a pointed look at Raesean before turning back to her father with a smile.

"See you in one week." She wiggled her fingers at everyone, then the screen went black.

"What happened?" Raesean asked.

"She cut the connection to the scrying spell," Selena mumbled.

"Do you think the demon level has locked everyone out?" Shalik asked.

"I don't think she's one to make idle threats," Abaddon said. As was his way, he'd remained silent throughout the exchange, probably gathering information and coming to conclusions based on what Evanora had said.

"I guess we'll be having a large dinner party soon, then," Shalik muttered. "Any idea what I should wear to a hostile dinner situation?"

Chapter 17

Selena lay in the boat, her face tilted up to the warm sun shining down on her. She relaxed as the lake water gently rocked it, carrying it further out into the center of the water.

It was quiet out here. No sounds of nature to cut into the silence. There were no animals in the surrounding area, no fish splashing in the water, and there certainly weren't any living beings enjoying the permanently beautiful day.

With the river of souls bleeding up onto Abaddon's level to create the lake, nothing alive could survive in it. In fact, very few living things could survive the Abyss. Except for rats, and those mutated creatures stayed in the pit. No, living things needed more than twilight, sulfur, and fire to survive. Nothing thrived down here except demons and people with Elysium blood—and now Shalik, it seemed.

So silence reigned, and she appreciated it.

The silence was the reason she was out here on the boat in the middle of the lake. Here she could calm her racing thoughts and get control of her magic. More importantly, she could finally analyze her emotions after the horrible mirror chat with her sister.

She had a sister, another member of her family she'd known nothing about, and just like when faced with a situation she couldn't control, she felt an uncontrollable rage. Her mother had not only abandoned her when she was a child but had hidden a sibling from her and a father.

A sibling who should have been raised well and cared for in a safe home, away from the scamming and dealmaking of the demon level. Her father had taken her there a few times when she was younger, and every time she'd visited, there'd been fighting and murder. How could a young girl grow up in a life like that?

It would explain why Evanora seems a little crazy when she speaks.

Selena sighed. She could only Imagine what her father was going through. To know the witch he loved had not only abandoned their family but had kept another child away from him. It made her angry all over again.

A shadow fell over her, blocking out the sun. She didn't bother opening her eyes to see what it was. Only something with wings could hover over her boat in the middle of the lake.

With a flutter of wings and a light bobbing of the boat, Reuel landed. "Fancy seeing you here."

Selena knew if she opened her eyes, she would see the angel's face smiling down at her. They'd done this so many times when she was younger, back before she became a Charon and saw the injustices of the world.

At that time, the two of them had been growing closer, and Selena had entertained dreams of becoming Reuel's wife. Even her father had noticed her infatuation with him. It was probably why he'd sent her to work as a Charon.

I guess there was a method to my father's madness.

If she hadn't gone to the surface world and met Mini and Shalik, her life might have taken a whole different turn. She would have been trapped down here, never knowing the truth.

"What are you thinking about so intently that you can't even acknowledge my presence?" Reuel asked.

Selena's eyes flew open, not only at his words but also at his tone. If she wanted to lie in her boat in silence, then it was her right to do so.

"Why do you need me to acknowledge your presence?" she snapped.

Reuel's eyes widened, not expecting her to respond the way she did.

"I'm sorry," he said. "I didn't mean to anger you. When I saw you in the boat, I just thought you wanted my company, but if you prefer to be alone, I understand."

Selena pressed her fingers to her eyes; her anger was getting the better of her. "No. I'm sorry. I just have a lot on my mind. It's been a difficult morning."

"Then I hope I can make it better." His citrine eyes lit up, and he shifted, allowing her to sit up.

"Maybe you can," she said with a smile she didn't feel. "Tell me about the souls that get to go to Elysium."

It was the ideal thing for her to say because the angel's face practically glowed as he talked about his perfect home and the perfect souls that get to live there. But all Selena could think about was how not perfect she was. She wasn't a calm, kind soul.

No. She was angry. Selena had loved and lost. There were parts of her that were still jagged from heartbreak and from the injustices of the surface world and in the Underworld.

She fingered the replica of her pendant around her neck, thinking about Raesean's words from the night before. The angel will never accept the broken parts of her because he doesn't know what it's like not to live in a perfect world.

He visited the Underworld every day, and yet he still couldn't comprehend that living beings were innately flawed creatures. As though her thoughts summoned him, Selena shifted her eyes to the shore to spot a familiar figure dressed in his signature white, hands in his pockets.

"Looks like I have to head back," she said, interrupting Reuel. She jerked her chin toward the shore.

The angel turned to see what she was looking at, and his body stiffened. "I guess you do."

Selena reached for the paddle, but Reuel laid a hand over it before she did. "Can I ask you something before you go?"

"Sure." She sat back, waiting for the angel to speak his mind.

"Are you involved with the demon?"

Selena rolled her lips together, fighting to get control of the rage spiking in her. "His name is Raesean, and no, I'm not, but if I were, what does it matter?"

Reuel shook his head as though he were looking at a naughty child. She wanted to push him overboard.

"Lena. He's a demon. You know what their kind is like. They're heartless beasts who thrive on chaos, destruction, deals, and financial gain. Being with him will only lead you to heartbreak, and I don't want to see that happen to you. You're too good for him."

"Tell me, Reuel. Are you saying this because you care about me or because you want us to pick up where we left off years ago?"

"Can't it be both?" He gave her hand a small squeeze.

"I'm not the young girl you once knew, Reuel," she whispered. "I'm not naïve, looking to stay home and be the little wife. My heart's been broken several times over, and of everyone in the world, only Raesean was there to help me pick up the pieces after the worst one."

Selena took a breath before she spoke the words that would no doubt hurt the angel. "I am also heir to the Underworld, Reuel. There's no part of our futures that allows me to be sitting at home waiting for you to return."

The angel pushed to his feet, looking down at her with hurt swimming in his eyes. "I see. Then I'll leave you to him."

Within seconds, his wings popped out and he was airborne, leaving Selena to row herself back to the shore.

Raesean watched every hard flap of the angel's wings as he crossed the sky. He didn't doubt Reuel was angry about something. Was it seeing him on the shore, or did Selena finally tell Mr. Perfect off? He knew which one he was hoping for.

He stood patiently while the oars cut through the calm water with every stroke she made closer to him. Reuel was lucky he'd left; otherwise, Raesean would have had to singe his wings for not being gentlemanly enough to row Selena back.

The boat neared, and he slipped off his shoes, wading into the water to help her drag it further on land.

"You'll get your suit wet," she pointed out, jumping out of the boat in the shorts and cropped T-shirt she'd donned to come out here in.

"It's fine," he gritted out, trying to ignore all that dark, silky flesh on display. "I have many others."

"Suit yourself."

They guided the boat inland, and then Selena scooped out the flip-flops inside while he picked up his own shoes.

"Were you looking for me?" she asked, heading to the walkway leading to the house.

"Your father sent me," he lied. "It's almost time for lunch, and then there is the dinner to plan."

"Humm."

Whether she knew he was lying, she didn't say. She just walked side by side with him into the house, and Raesean had no problem with that.

"This is going to be a disaster," Raesean said to Abaddon and Selena after lunch.

The plan for the dinner with Evanora and Belial lay on scattered sheets of paper all over Abaddon's desk. The three of them had gone over everything they could think of, from security and seating arrangements to appetizers and music.

Selena suggested they put some mirrors on the doors and spell them so that anyone who wanted to cause harm that night couldn't enter, and Raesean thought it was a brilliant idea. But even with all their precautions, Raesean still thought things were going to go wrong.

Selena rolled her eyes at him. "Of course it's going to be a disaster. Evanora is a wildcard, and Belial is an unknown factor who could either try to kill us on the spot or use this soiree to set us up to get killed in the future."

"The problem is," Raesean said, ignoring Selena's sarcasm, "there are two major unestablished factors in this. One is we don't exactly know what they want. The other being, what weapon are they going to use to try to kill you?"

His gaze shifted to Abaddon. He knew the being was hiding something, and he'd waited long enough for the king of the Underworld to show his cards. They couldn't afford to wait any longer.

Abaddon swirled the well-aged whiskey in his glass, gaze locked on him. Raesean just waited him out until he emptied the glass, then slammed it down on his desktop.

"There's a dagger."

Selena cursed under her breath, pinching the bridge of her nose. Another time, Raesean would have found the gesture cute, but there were other important things to focus on. Such as blades that could kill someone from Elysium. Which means they could kill anyone.

"What is this dagger, and where did it come from?"

"It's mine," Abaddon sighed, his eyes taking on a distant look. "When your mother and I first got together, Selena, she played this game called "what if." She would ask the most random questions. What if she got old? What if I fell in love with someone else? I knew what she was doing. She was insecure about our relationship and, in an odd way, was seeking reassurance that I really wanted to spend the rest of my life with her."

"What does that have to do with your dagger?"

Abaddon shot Raesean a hard look, and he reclined in the visitor's chair in front of Abaddon's desk.

"As I was saying, she wanted to be reassured. When I came down from Elysium, I had a dagger that was specially made. It could kill anything except me. If I were to be stabbed in the heart by it, I'd fall into a sleep for a hundred years."

"A hundred years is a long time for you not to be in charge of the Underworld," Raesean pointed out. "A lot could happen in that time."

Abaddon shrugged.

"So you gave Mom the dagger to declare your love, and she left with it," Selena confirmed.

"That's the stupidest thing you could have done," Selena and Raesean said in unison.

Abaddon threw back his head and laughed. "How did I manage to raise two such jaded people?"

"Raise?" Selena glanced between him and her father. Raesean shifted in his seat, brushing imaginary lint from his pant leg.

"I think we should focus on..."

"He was such a tiny thing when I first found him on the streets of the demon level," Abaddon said with a teasing glint in his eyes.

At his words, Raesean could practically smell the sulfur that would choke you while you lived there. The longer you lived on that level, the more accustomed you became to it, but even after so many years, he could never forget the smell.

"He was fierce though," Abaddon continued. "When he couldn't get what he wanted with charm, he would do it with his fist or a blade."

Selena gave Raesean an appraising look he wasn't sure he liked, and he racked his brain, trying to figure out how to derail this conversation. He wasn't ashamed of his past. He just didn't enjoy talking about it. It was his past, and it should stay there, not stir pitying looks from people he cared about.

"What happened next?" Selena asked. She leaned forward from her seat in the visitor's chair next to his. Raesean looked at her father with daggers in his eyes, and the king of the Underworld smiled at him, prepared to torture him. He shouldn't have expected anything else.

"First, he tried to relieve me of several valuable items. When he failed, he threatened to slit my throat."

"What?" Selena said with a chuckle. "Didn't he know who you were?"

"In my defense, I was living on the streets, and it's not like the upper demons shared information with runts like me."

The two of them only looked at him with matching smiles. They were so alike it was a wonder he didn't immediately know who she was the moment he saw her.

"I saw the determination in him and brought him home. Then I trained him to be my right hand."

Selena frowned. "Wait, he lives here?"

"Lived," Abaddon clarified. "He bought that fancy apartment on the surface that he refused to furnish. But I still keep his room here as he likes it. Almost as sparse as his apartment."

"Why should I furnish it? Between the club and here, I'm never there. Not to mention, leaving personal effects around when you have so many enemies is like putting a target on the backs of the people you care about."

Abaddon scoffed.

"So why didn't I know about you before I went to the surface world?" Selena asked.

"By the time you came along, he was already doing my bidding on the surface. He hardly ever came home to visit after that."

"Great," Raesean cut in. "Now you know the story. Can we get back to the issue at hand? With one shot, Belial could send you into a hundred-year sleep."

Selena nodded, but he knew she was going to revisit this topic when he wasn't around.

"He can't," Abaddon said, interrupting his thoughts.

"I thought you said..."

"No one can wield the blade if they aren't born with Elysium blood. I was sentimental, not crazy."

"There's the non-trusting ruler of the Underworld that I know," Raesean murmured with a smile.

"So if Belial can't do it," Selena mused, "then that means..."

"Yes, your sister is the one who's going to have to stab me in the heart."

Chapter 18

There was something that had plagued her ever since the meeting with Raesean and her father earlier today.

At first, she hadn't known what it was, and she'd gone about her busy evening of showing Shalik around the property. He'd gone crazy in Abaddon's vegetable garden, and Selena knew she had to be on the lookout for his next vegetable concoction.

But the unsettling feeling festered in the hours that passed right up until dinner, when the subject of her sister had come up again. Her father had chosen her to be heir because she was his only daughter, but now there was another.

Would he want her to rule the Underworld instead? Granted, she was batshit crazy, but maybe if she spent more time with them, she could fully understand that what happened to her wasn't their fault.

Selena had chewed on the thought throughout dinner, and now, she was sitting in her father's office, watching him review reports from the few demons still loyal to him. Raesean had gone to the demon level to gather as much information on the lockdown Evanora had mentioned. Thus far, they had heard no updates from him.

If Evanora knew what was good for her, she would ensure Rae returned in one piece.

Selena frowned at the thought. When did Raesean become a being she cared about?

"What's wrong?" her father asked, scratching something with a pen in the document's margin.

"Why do you think something is wrong? I'm fine."

She sunk her teeth into her bottom lip, shifting her gaze to Cerberus snoring in the corner. She felt like she hadn't seen the dog for the entire day. He had probably been running around somewhere with his siblings.

"You're sitting there quietly," Abaddon said, bringing her back to their conversation. "With a frown on your face, chewing on your lip. In the past, you would at least be listening to music or reading a book."

She rolled her eyes at him.

"Are you worried about Raesean? He'll be back soon, and then you two can resume whatever you have going on together."

"What?" Selena sputtered. "There's nothing going on between us, and I'm not worried about him."

Her father lowered the paper in his hand, arched his brow, and tilted his head. "Nothing going on between you two? That demon watches your every move with more hunger in his eyes than Cerberus does when he sees his treats."

As if to highlight his point, Cerberus perked up, ears pointed, a big smile on his face. "Not you," Abaddon told the hopeful dog. Cerberus sneezed, as though to show his displeasure, rolled over, and then went back to sleep.

"It's not like that." Selena toyed with the necklace Raesean had given her as a replacement. "Well, I don't think it's like that anymore. At first, I didn't want to date him because he was a demon, and I didn't want him to tell you where I was. Then, when everything with Mini happened, we, err... had a discussion."

"Is that what they are calling it these days? A discussion?"

Selena ducked her face, not wanting her father to see her embarrassment. "It's not what you're thinking. Anyway, he cut all ties with me, but then we came down here, and things have been all muddled."

"Hum. I think you both need to get out of your heads, but you guys are adults, and I'm sure you will work things out," Abaddon said. "Now, if you're not worried about Raesean, then what's bothering you?"

"Evanora," Selena blurted.

"What about her?"

"I know you only chose me because I was your only heir, but now you have two daughters..." She trailed off.

Abaddon leaned back in his chair and linked his hands over his stomach. "You're worried I would want Evanora to replace you."

"She seems dedicated to the Underworld, and I abandoned my position the first chance I got." Selena tugged at a loose thread on her sweatshirt.

"What you're saying is I should give the keys to the Underworld to someone being used as a puppet by demons instead of to you, who would fight Elysium so that lesser beings' souls are accepted down here."

She nodded.

He shook his head. "I don't know where you get these notions from, but at least you're talking to me about them now. You weren't chosen to be my heir because you are my only daughter. I could have chosen any being from Elysium to be my heir. But I'd rather not have the souls and demons down here suffer if they don't need to.

"*That's* why I chose you. Even though you try to hide it, a part of you will always support the lesser beings, and I think it's time someone does. I cannot because I am bound by Elysium's rules. And even though I've only just met her, I don't think your sister will make a good ruler. She's too temperamental."

Selena swiped at the tear threatening to fall. "I'm sorry I abandoned you without a word."

"And I'm sorry you believed you couldn't come to me and ask to see the surface world."

Selena smiled. "To be honest, I didn't realize I wanted to live up there until I started seeing the other beings when I went to collect souls."

"Oh, so I put myself in this position," Abaddon teased, and she laughed.

Selena stood, brushing out imaginary wrinkles from her sweatshirt and leggings. She walked around her father's desk and wrapped her arms around his neck. "I'm glad to be home."

"Even though I missed you, I'm glad you learned more about the surface world. It's only going to make you a better leader for everyone down here, and I'm proud of how mature you've become."

She pulled away, unsure of what to say.

Abaddon cleared his throat. "Now, off to bed. You're going to need as much rest as possible over the next few days."

Selena headed for the door.

"And Lena?"

"Yes?" She looked over her shoulder at her father.

"Try to figure things out with the demon soon. Sometimes, you need a partner to help keep you from going insane."

Her mouth dropped open, but she remained speechless.

Did her father just encourage her to date Raesean?

The demon in her bed was warm and smelled of sulfur. She didn't have to open her eyes to see who it was because under the smell of sulfur was the masculine scent that was just Raesean. Besides, she had been waking up to him in her bed the last few days, no matter how much she told him to stop it.

She supposed if he wanted to be in her bed, she might as well take advantage of the body heat. Snuggling closer, she pulled the covers tighter around her and tried to go back to sleep.

"Shouldn't you be waking up instead of burrowing down to sleep longer?"

"I see no reason I should wake up. Today is going to be a horrible day, and I think I should just sit this one out."

Raesean ran a hand up her back and into her hair, leaving a trail of heat that wormed its way into her blood and headed straight for her lower regions.

"My vicious creature, I've never known you to be a coward."

Selena's eyes flew open, and she jabbed her elbow into his stomach. He let out a soft *umph* as she pushed away from him.

"There's the vicious creature I know." He propped his head on his hand and looked down at her. "There's no use trying to avoid the inevitable. The dinner party is tonight, and there is still a lot to prepare."

"I'm sure Chaim has it well in hand. Elysium knows if I try to do anything, he might keel over and die."

"I think he's sturdy enough to withstand you checking in on him. Besides, we will have to go over all the security measures and what you need to do should they attack."

"I can protect myself. I just want to make sure Shalik is safe. Evanora and Belial know just where to hit to hurt."

Raesean pulled her close, resuming his ministrations. "Shalik knows to head right back to his room with Cerberus should our carefully executed dinner fall apart."

"Good. Evanora might be my sister by blood, but Shalik is my family. The last remaining member of the family I made when I went to the surface world, and I don't think I could handle losing him right now."

"I know. It's why I've drilled into him several times what he needs to do."

Selena sighed, both from the feel of Raesean's fingers on her scalp and from the thoughts about the dinner. "Do you think my sister will really stab our father in the heart?"

"I'm not sure. I think a part of her wants to be acknowledged by your father, and that's why she's demanding this elaborate event. But the bitter part of her wants to rule in his stead because she thinks the demons are being treated unjustly."

"I haven't been down to the demon level since I was little. Do you think she's right?"

There was a beat or two of silence as though he was weighing his words. "I think some demons are treated unfairly. The ones who don't have power strong enough to fight back. Ultimately,

I believe that Belial just wants an excuse to rule the Underworld and cause chaos on the surface."

"Demons who don't have a lot of power like the pit demons," Selena said.

"Yes. As you aptly pointed out on our trip here, many creatures are born into the life they have. Not all of them want to stay in that life."

"So there are other demons who just want a change in their lives, not to cause destruction on the surface."

"I met a few of them when I snuck into the demon level."

Selena bolted upright. "You got in?"

He nodded. "Your sister is good with her magic and her spells, but she's not as good as you."

"What did you find out?"

"The demons who side with General Belial are mostly from his demon army. Many are neutral and are going along with the plan until they see who the winner is. Then there are the ones who want a different life but don't agree with what Belial is doing. They want to experience the surface world and live peacefully if they can."

"After this is over, maybe I should start looking into how my father can implement some changes."

"Humm," he said, scrubbing a hand through his bed hair. The muscles in his exposed abs flexed with the movement, and Selena sunk her teeth into her bottom lip as she admired the view.

Her gaze drifted up the hard plains of his body to his full lips and, at last, his blue eyes that sparkled with mirth. "Enjoying what you see?"

"Very much so," she replied, raking her gaze over his body once more.

"You can do more than watch." He slid closer, untangling his lower half from the blanket they slept under. "You can touch and taste too. I'm sure you'd definitely enjoy savoring."

Raesean leaned in and brushed his lips over hers. A soft kiss and a promise that whenever she wanted him, she could have him.

"Can I ask you something?" she asked instead.

"Yes," he said as he planted another kiss on her lips.

"Why did you cut ties with me last year after everything went down?"

He pulled away, taking all the heat he'd generated with him.

"Since the moment I laid eyes on you, I've wanted you."

Selena sucked in a breath at his revelation.

"Then I found out who your father was, and I thought you were planning something against him, and that's why you were on the surface world. That's why you avoided all demons like your life depended on it." He rubbed the back of his neck. "It never occurred to me you were running from your father and your position in the Abyss. I believed that one day I would have to choose a side, and I wasn't sure I could choose between the man who raised me and... you."

Selena reached up her hand to smooth some of the hair that refused to lay flat. "And now?"

"After watching you, spending time with you, and learning your heart, I know if I had to choose, I would be by your side, saving the world or burning it to the ground."

Chapter 19

If I had to choose, I would be by your side, saving the world or burning it to the ground.

Raesean's words echoed in Selena's head for the rest of the day. While she was with the Sacrodaemon chef reviewing the menu for the dinner, she basked in the warm feeling it gave her. When she checked in with Chaim to ensure everything in the dining room was set up, her heart skipped a beat at the thought of them. Even when she was going through the safety measures with the security, she had to fight back a smile at the thought of him.

He would choose her.

Not because she was to take her father's place and rule the Underworld at her side or because she had powerful magic that many coveted. Even after he said he'd wanted nothing to do with her, he kept watch, learned about her, looked at her flaws, the darkness growing in her, and still wanted to be by her side.

No one has ever accepted all of her like that. The good and the bad. Even her father expected her to make a change for the better, and she wanted that. To help the lesser beings who didn't have a place in the Underworld. Many on the surface world who heard about her magic thought she was the benevolent witch prophesied to bring change every five hundred years.

But her magic wasn't kind and merciful; it couldn't do what people wanted and transfer magic from one being to another. Raesean knew this and still wanted to be with her, even though a part of her thrived on death and power. Taking a soul from another gave her magic that power. Gave it the strength to have every being kneeling before her in fear of their lives because she could hold their soul in the palms of her hands.

Selena shook herself, pushing away the dark path her thoughts had taken. She needed to be more vigilant these days, as her abilities had gotten a taste of death. She could feel them growing, demanding she feed them.

Taking a deep breath, she settled her mind as she made her way down the hallway to her room. They'd removed all the mirrors that were usually in the halls and repurposed them to the different entrances of the manor. She'd used them to create a protection spell to prevent anyone from entering the manor who wished harm against any living being here.

As she neared her room, she mentally went over the spell she'd used, looking for any loopholes. It wouldn't do to have her sister outsmart her during this dinner. It might be a fatal mistake.

The sound of music coming out of Shalik's room had her knocking on his door.

"Come in."

She pushed the door open. Shalik sat cross-legged on his bed, scribbling in a notebook, music flowing from his phone.

It might as well be used for something down here.

"What are you doing?" she asked, snatching the book from his hand.

"Hey." He grabbed it back before she could even read its contents. "If you must know, Miss Nosy, I'm working on some new potion recipes and adjusting some old ones to include your father's vegetables. Did you know some of them can't even be found on the surface world?"

Selena rolled her eyes at him, though inside she was smiling. She hadn't seen him this excited about potion-making since before Mini's death. "You and my father need to stop this obsession with vegetables."

"Those vegetables are sometimes key in the potions I make, which means that I need them so we can make our customers happy," Shalik pointed out, making another notation in his book.

"How are you going to make potions with these rare vegetables when we go back to Fusion City?"

Shalik looked up at her, slamming the book shut. "We're going back?"

Selena paused, watching the panicked look on her friend's face. She moved further into the room and lowered next to him. "You don't want to go back?"

He shrugged, looking away from her. "I didn't really think about it until you mentioned it just now. I just thought, since you're no longer running from your dad and you're planning to take over from him, that you would stay down here for a while."

Selena took the book from him and placed it on the bed. "If you're not ready to go back, then we'll stay, and when you're ready, then we'll go. Whatever you decide, I'll go with you because you're more than my friend, Shalik. You're my family, and we have to stick together."

He reached over, dragging her to him, clutching her close. A tremor racked through his body, and the moisture dampened her thin T-shirt. Selena held him tighter as the tears continued to flow.

Selena left Shalik, hopefully healed more than how he was before he came here. If they were back in their apartment in Fusion City, they would have probably gathered all the junk food they could find and settled in to watch movies for the rest of the night. Waking up in the morning with an upset stomach but feeling emotionally better.

In the Abyss, however, they both had to prepare for a dinner with volatile personalities, one of them being crazy to top it off.

Stepping into her room, she closed the door behind her before noticing the big white box on the bed. She searched the room for any exposed mirrors or anyone waiting to pounce before she approached the box. On the top, there was a cream-colored card. When she flipped it over, she smiled.

"Lena, I know you had something else in mind for tonight, but I thought this might be more appropriate as it won't show blood should you decide to spill any tonight. R."

Laying the card on the bed, she opened the box.

Nestled inside was the most gorgeous dress she'd ever seen. She reached in and lifted the delicate confection out. The fabric was a rich mixture of blood red flowing into darker tones. It crisscrossed into intricate designs, leaving holes that would expose a lot of skin. There were two high slits on either side, and she could envision how much leg she was going to be showing.

Trust Raesean to know exactly what would match her mood today. She couldn't wait to see how it fit. Laying the dress out on the bed, she checked the time. She needed to hurry if she was going to be ready for the guests.

An evil grin tugged at the corners of her lips. At least she'd be looking damn good when they arrived.

Raesean stood outside Selena's door and sucked in a deep breath. He clenched and unclenched his fists, trying to stop the tremor in his hands. He couldn't figure out why they were shaking.

He'd known Selena for years. And especially the last year—unbeknownst to her, he would sneak into her room just to check on her. He knew her better than she knew herself.

Then why can't I just knock on her door?

Giving himself an inner shake, he forced his knuckles to connect with the hardwood in three successive raps that almost sounded angry.

"Just a minute," she called out. Her smoky voice caused a wave of goosebumps to travel over his skin. That random feeling should have been enough to warn him.

Who was he kidding? Nothing could have prepared him for the vision before him who opened the door. She was probably the angel who started the war in Elysium.

Just as he thought it would, the crisscrossed swathes of fabric hugged her every curve and played peek-a-boo with the skin of her stomach and the tops of her high, curvy breasts. The high slits on both sides of the dress exposed miles of creamy leg, and Raesean couldn't wait to have her walk in front of him in that dress.

"Well?" Selena arched a brow, then did a little spin in the doorway. Raesean stifled a groan when he noticed the back was just as delicious as the front. "What do you think?"

Realizing that he'd stood there like a speechless fool for the last three minutes, he cleared his throat.

"You look stunning, Selena."

The smile she gave him. He was sure lesser beings had gone to war for one like it, and, truth be told, he would probably do the same.

"Thank you, but where did you get it?" she asked, running delicate fingers over the airy fabric. He wanted her to run her fingers over him that way just before ripping that damn dress off of her.

He'd made a mistake with his selection. How was he supposed to concentrate on the importance of tonight if she was walking around looking like every male's perfect fantasy?

"Are you sure it's not too much?"

Raesean realized he was staring again and slid one hand into his pocket before he reached out and started something neither one of them could indulge in at the moment. And indulge is exactly what he was going to do the moment he had her alone. He would peel that dress off and let his mouth and hands cover every part of her skin. Then he would feast.

"Maybe I should change."

"Don't you dare. If anyone is removing that dress from you, it's going to be me. Slowly, so I can take my time pleasuring you."

Her breath caught, and he was glad she realized what she was doing to him. "You look exactly like who you are in that dress,

Selena. Like an angel—one you'll get on your knees to worship, even though you know the angel has fallen and will take you to the Abyss."

Her tongue darted out to taste her red-slicked lips, and he wanted to replace them with his own.

"I... I think we should head to dinner," she muttered. Her breath was coming out in soft pants, and the demon in him wondered how it would sound if he sexually tortured her, denying her that release until she was begging for it.

"Yes," he agreed, shutting down the lava of desire that was flowing through him. "Let's head to the dining room. We can't afford to be distracted this evening."

He held out his elbow for her, and she slid an arm through, closing the bedroom door behind her. Before they moved, he leaned in and whispered in her ear. "I want you to remember where this conversation paused because we'll definitely be picking up where we left off later."

A shiver racked through her body, and Raesean smiled. He thought he'd wanted her to come to him, but maybe seducing her might be more pleasurable for both of them.

Chapter 20

Abaddon and Shalik were already in the dining room when they entered, and so was the angel. Raesean felt absolute satisfaction, with a large dose of pettiness, when the angel looked at him and his eyes hardened. If looks could kill, then Raesean would have been bleeding out on the ground by now.

Then Reuel's eyes shifted to Selena on his arm, and for the second time tonight, he thought he'd made a mistake. The angel's citrine eyes blazed with lust as his gaze traveled from the delicate curls that Selena had pinned up to expose her lovely neck to the matching slippers she'd chosen to wear instead of heels.

The demon wanted to carve the angel's eyes out for looking at her that way. Reuel's wings fluttered—the involuntary reaction a sure sign that he wasn't having pure thoughts about Selena right now. If the angel wasn't careful, he was going to be a fallen one, and Raesean would enjoy introducing him to life on the demon level or in the pit.

"Reuel," Selena said, moving them further into the dining room when all Raesean wanted to do was cover her in his suit jacket so the angel would stop eye fucking her.

"I didn't know you were going to be here tonight."

"Technically, he's not," Abaddon said, eyeing the trio with an amused look. "But I want him to be nearby should things go awry. He's the only one I can trust to take a message back to Elysium."

Translation: If the shit hits the fan, then Reuel will let the higher-ups know that they need to send someone to take care of this little coup.

Selena looked at her father, and Raesean wasn't sure what emotion crossed her face, but she squared her shoulders. "Then let's stick to the plan and not have Reuel make such a long flight tonight."

"I second that notion," Shalik said. He lifted the glass of champagne he was sipping as though giving a toast.

"Now that we're all in agreement, I believe the angel needs to leave before our guests arrive, and we all need to be prepared for the night's events," Raesean said.

He gave Reuel a small smirk as though to drive the point of him being unwanted home. Instead of taking the hint, the angel put away his wings and stepped closer to him.

"You might be on the upper levels, Raesean, but everyone falls eventually."

Raesean's smile widened, and he lifted his hand to brush imaginary lint off the angel's sleeve. "Even angels like you, Reuel."

For the second time that evening, he had to thank the higher powers that looks couldn't kill. The angel slapped his hand away, storming out of the dining room.

"I really need to work on having popcorn at the ready whenever you three are in the same room," Shalik said, sampling one of the hors d'oeuvres. "You always bring such entertainment. It's like watching a movie."

"Glad we could be of amusement to you," Selena muttered, snatching up her own glass of champagne and taking a deep drink.

"Careful, or you might end up drunk before the guests arrive." Raesean slid his hands over her wrist before wrapping his fingers around the glass she held. "It would be a shame for you to be too drunk to enjoy the after-party."

Her lips parted on a soft breath, and her tongue darted out to slick over the red she painted them. The motion captivated him, and he wanted to follow the movement with his own tongue. Maybe they should just skip the party altogether.

"Ahem." Someone cleared their throat, breaking the spell between them and forcing him to take a step back from her. It wouldn't do to forget why they were having this dinner.

He had people to protect, and climbing into bed with one of them would not help.

"Selena, why don't you stand over here with me? The pair of you look about ready to combust," Shalik suggested, hooking an arm through Selena's. She scowled at him but allowed him to put some distance between her and Raesean.

Raesean took a few steps to stand at Abaddon's side, looking over the ruler's dark, impeccable suit and red shirt, no tie. His signature colors. When he thought about it, Selena used to wear red as well when she'd first come to Fusion City.

She'd worn it less and less the more she came into her own. Then, not at all when she started her own club. She began wearing more silver and blues, playing into her mirror witch status.

He supposed he shouldn't be surprised that she knew how to project a certain image to people. After all, she probably learned it at her father's knee. Raesean looked down at his own suit. He didn't wear red. With his unnaturally pale skin, he would look like a candy cane if he did, so he wore a white one.

Raesean loved playing into the angelic look of purity that many people think of when they see white. When he was young and his enemies saw him coming, they would think he would show them mercy. Until it was too late, because sometimes the deadliest creatures looked the purest. His ruthless ways had earned him the nickname *wraith*. He was like a curse upon his enemies.

Over the years, his reputation had preceded him, so he could afford to be less ruthless, and he'd enjoy not having to slaughter so many. He'd hoped to continue his track record of not having to return to that persona, but tonight was different.

Belial and Evanora were threatening things dear to him, and he would gladly don that white suit and splatter it with blood to protect them.

"What are you thinking that has you so pensive?" Abaddon asked, bringing him out of his thoughts.

"Just thinking of what you've taught me over the years about instilling fear in others."

"Sounds like you're bringing out the wraith once again," Abaddon said, eerily guessing the direction of his thoughts.

"Yes," he said. "He's ready to play."

There was a soft sound of shattered glass, the sound Selena had attached to her spell as an indicator that their guests were here.

It was time.

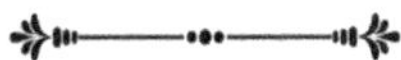

The sound of shattering glass had Selena gripping Shalik's arm. "Remember the plan, Shalik. Keep Cerberus at your side, and if you see things are going to shit, get the hell out."

Shalik gave her a nod. Selena moved to step away from him, but he kept his hand tight on hers. "Whatever you do, Selena, survive. I mean it."

She gave his hand another squeeze, then stepped away from him.

"Miss Selena, the guests have arrived, but some of them are unable to enter the premises," Chaim said.

"I guess the spell I cast is working," Selena said with a fierce smile.

Raesean moved to her side and whispered, "Such a vicious creature."

She stole a look at him, goosebumps breaking out over her skin at the heated look he was giving her.

"Let's go greet your father's guests," Raesean said with a glance over his shoulder at the king of the Underworld.

"I think that's a great idea," Abaddon said, adjusting the sleeves of his suit, leading the way. Selena and Raesean fell into step behind him as he strolled through the dining room doors, heading to the main ones.

When they got to the main door, it was propped wide open, and one of the demons was pounding on an invisible force. Selena couldn't help the thrill of satisfaction that went through her.

Her sister must not be as powerful as she pretended to be; otherwise, she would have been able to break the spell.

"What seems to be the problem here?" Abaddon paused on the other side of the doorway, where the unknown demon was pounding on the invisible force.

"It seems you've brought us here under false pretenses." The voice was deep and gravelly as the being who spoke stepped forward so Selena could get a better look at him. He was tall, with smooth skin tinged an unusual shade of yellow. His shoulders were broad, and it had Selena wondering how he fit through narrow doorways. His head had no hair and reflected any light that came in his direction.

Selena could see why he'd been a general in the Underworld army for so long. If she were a demon, she wouldn't want to be at the mercy of his thick, meaty hands either.

"Yes. I planned an entire dinner under false pretenses, just for fun." Abaddon's tone was drier than towels out of the laundry, and it certainly lacked the fun, fluffy aspect. "I don't have time for this show that you and your minions are about to put on. Do you really think I would give you free rein in my home?"

Belial scanned everyone who stood in the doorway with her father, then grinned, showing off sharp, pointed teeth. "All these precautions. Don't you trust me?"

"The rules are simple," Abaddon said, not acknowledging the taunt. "Anyone who wishes harm to anyone in residence here can't enter."

The sharp sound of palm against palm split the night, and Selena shifted her gaze to look at her sister. Evanora slipped between the demons standing behind Belial. She wore Abaddon's signature red in a formfitting sleeveless tube dress that clung to all of her curves. She had gained a few inches of height with the matching red stilettos she'd paired it with.

"It seems your magic is stronger than I thought," her sister said, a smirk playing across her lips.

"Something you should never forget." Selena moved to stand at her father's side.

"Had I known this, I would have taken a different approach to the evening."

"I don't care what approach you would have taken," her father cut in. "The rules remain. Anyone who wishes to pass this threshold can't desire to cause harm to any of its residents."

Abaddon slid his hands into the pockets of his suit pants, much like Raesean, who stood quietly observing everything. Selena wondered if the mannerism was also something he picked up from her father.

"Let's compromise then," Evanora said. She moved closer to Belial so that she mirrored Selena's pose with her father. "No one entering your little home will cause its residents harm *tonight*. I can't really promise for the future."

Selena eyed her sister, knowing she was missing something. The witch was too confident in her words and willing to compromise too quickly.

Silence rippled through the group as Selena turned over the careful way her sister acquiesced.

"Selena?" Her father's voice jarred the faint suspicion from her mind.

"Yes?" She turned to him.

"Allow them in, but through this doorway only."

She gave him a brief nod, then stepped back to adjust her spell on the mirror. Once done, she moved back to her father's side.

"Only four of you can enter, and the one who'd been trying to get past the barrier isn't allowed. Decide carefully among yourselves who's going to enter because my daughter added a little twist to the mirror if you mean us any harm, and I don't think you want to find out what it is."

Raesean leaned over and whispered in her ear, "Vicious creature."

Selena bit back a smile. This was no time to be grinning. They were about to let in two demons with powers she didn't know about, the general of the demon army, and a mirror witch with a chip on her shoulder because she had daddy issues.

Selena wasn't a betting witch, but if she was, she would drop several gold coins on the night ending in bloodshed. She would make a fortune. This entire situation was a bomb with a timer on it, waiting to explode.

Chapter 21

The debate between Belial and Evanora was intense as they went back and forth on which of their minions would enter with them. After several minutes of debating, they finally chose two of the demons to enter the manor.

Belial stepped cautiously across the threshold as though he expected something to jump out and impale him. He stood in front of the mirror placed on the door and waited while the mirror judged his intentions. When he'd made it safely to the other side, he shot Selena a triumphant look.

Her sister followed, sauntering in with no fear marring her perfectly made-up face. She gave a shallow curtsy, and Selena rolled her eyes at the pair. The first demon to join them came through the doorway with a stoic expression that Selena appreciated. She'd grown tired of the charade.

Then came the last demon. Unfortunately, he hadn't been honest about his intentions because the moment he crossed the threshold and stood in front of the mirror, her spell kicked in, freezing him in place.

"What did you do?" Belial demanded, reaching a hand out to touch the popsicle demon.

"I warned you, my daughter added a special surprise to her spell," Abaddon smirked at Belial, who had clearly tried to sneak in someone who would have attempted to kill them before the night was over. "You're lucky she didn't have him sliced into ribbons."

Belial's yellow skin turned a mottled red as he balled his hands into fists.

"Don't lose your head just yet." Evanora laid a hand on his arm. "I'm sure the effects will wear off soon. Besides, it's his fault for lying about his intentions for the evening. Let's get the others to cart him out and replace him."

As if on cue, Chaim, the head Sacrodaemon servant, wheeled in a dolly to put the frozen demon on. Selena would have laughed if she thought it wouldn't have angered Belial more. She was trying her best to get the evening over without spilling blood.

Once they carted the demon out and replaced him, everyone took their seats at the dining table. The soft music the Sacrodaemon played through the speakers pushed against the thick tension in the room. Everyone was keeping their gaze on each other as though, at any moment, magic was going to fly and they would have to defend themselves.

Porcelain clinked as the servants placed the first round of food in front of the guests. It was enough to have everyone looking away from each other.

It was a thin, yellow split pea soup garnished with basil leaves and steaming hot. Selena picked up her spoon and sampled the well-seasoned concoction. She couldn't help the smile that lit up her face as memories of eating this in the kitchen while the chef prepared other meals came back to her.

"That good?" Evanora's voice changed her smile into a scowl as she looked across the table at her sister. They'd separated the table in half, with Belial and his party sitting on one side and Abaddon and his sitting on the other.

Abaddon had given up his usual place at the head of the table so that if he needed to get rid of the general, no one was in his way. He wanted a clear target for a blade or magic if need be.

"Is this a favorite of yours?" Evanora continued to probe, and Selena was giving up on the soup.

"Yes, if you must know."

Her sister slipped a spoonful past her lips, her tongue darting out to catch a stray drop. She hummed her appreciation as though she were having an intimate moment with the soup.

"Delicious."

Selena pushed the bowl away from her, her appetite ruined. "Do you plan to sound like a porn star after every bite you take? If so, let me know so I can tell the chef to keep a plate warm for me in the kitchen."

"I don't know what you mean?" Evanora said, eyes wide, trying to convey innocence.

"She's pointing out the very obscene sounds you were making over the soup you were using to get a rise out of her." Shalik arched a brow at Evanora, and she scowled back at him. "While I'm all for siblings poking fun at each other, the rest of us would like to eat our food in peace without hearing a banshee in heat."

Evanora's hands tightened around the spoon, and she gave him that manic smile that Selena realized was her signal that she was plotting evil and dangerous things.

"Don't even think about it," she warned her sister. Her power surged upward, the need to protect her best friend as vital as her next breath. The darkness of her magic slithered through her veins, calling out to every reflective surface in the room. Everything trembled, then paused like a lung-filled breath, waiting for her to breathe out and unleash her fury.

To the pit with peaceful talks, Selena absolutely would not lose Shalik to someone who just wanted to be petty.

A warm hand slid up her thigh, tempering the darkness in her. "Such a vicious creature, but there's nothing she can do to harm him at this moment," Raesean whispered to her.

His words were like a healing balm over a raw wound, calming the ferocious rage, pulling her out of the darkness that kept sucking her down. Selena let out a breath, reeling in the magic so that the sharp edges receded, tucking itself back into the deep pit inside of her where it lay ready to be summoned.

"Do you have so little control over your power?" Belial's words almost had her magic pouncing out of her again.

Raesean took a sip of his wine before he gave Belial a smug look. "Of course, at *your* power level, you wouldn't understand the amount of skill needed to prevent it from spilling over and killing everyone."

The demon waved away Raesean's words with his meaty hand, the flesh rippling with the movement. "Nora has the same power as her, yet you don't see the cutlery flying about whenever she's in a snit."

"Evanora can't even dream of having the same level of power. If she did, she would have been able to break the simple spell on the mirrors in the doorway," Raesean pointed out.

The cracking of glass had Selena looking over at the witch in question, who was holding the remains of her wineglass in her fist. The contents of the glass and her blood decorated the table like a morbid abstract painting. Sacrodaemon servants rushed forward to clean up the mess Evanora made, efficiently mopping up the blood, removing the glass fragments, bandaging her hand, and even removing her place setting and replacing her soup.

"I guess Selena isn't the only one who has a temper problem," Abaddon commented. He pushed away his empty bowl, probably not missing a spoonful of his meal during the entire exchange. "Now that we've traded insults and showed off all our powers, let's get to the business at hand. What do you want, Belial?"

The Sacrodaemons took his word as a cue to clear the table and bring out the next course—a mini salad with crisp greens and a vinaigrette dressing. Selena picked at the tomatoes and cucumbers while she waited for her father and his general to finish their staring contest.

As expected, Belial broke first. "The demons are unhappy in the Underworld. They want more freedom to roam the surface world."

"Elysium law states only a certain amount of you can roam above. To do so, you must still have a tether so I can monitor what you are doing. Do you presume to break that rule?"

"Yes, I do. I want my people happy, and the noose around their neck has to go." Belial took the last bite of his salad, his thick fingers dabbing at his mouth with the white linen napkin. "You've sat on the throne for millennia, and you've done nothing for the lives of the beings down here. Your reign is over."

Abaddon laid down his salad fork. His gaze was hard as he looked at the general in front of him. "You don't want freedom for the demons. You want a war with Elysium."

The entire room fell silent. Not even Cerberus moved as all eyes fell on Belial in horror at what he wanted to do.

"I don't know what you mean." He crossed his wide arms over his chest and rocked back in his chair. Selena shifted her gaze to Evanora and saw the same horror reflected in her. I guess Belial hadn't told her his entire plan.

"You can't be serious," Raesean growled, his own salad forgotten. "A war with Elysium would never stay contained down here. It would spill over into the human world, and then they would decimate everything that isn't..."

He trailed off. "That's what you want. A three-way war between the humans and angels. You want to rule over every living being out there.

"Millions would die, and the humans would never allow you to sit on your own throne. They would destroy the world first, and those beings whose souls aren't allowed into the Underworld would be extinguished. They would be eradicated."

"Less creatures who would turn their nose up at us," Belial responded with a sneer. "They've treated demons as the scum of the earth for too long. It's time we show the world who we are."

"You never wanted to negotiate, did you?" Selena whispered.

Evanora scoffed. "Of course not. I can't believe a witch like you would be so gullible you would believe that."

Belial laid a hand on Evanora's, silencing her, then looked at Abaddon. "If you hand over the role as king of the Underworld to Evanora, we'll let you return to Elysium to share the good news with them."

"And if I don't?"

"Then I'll return with the demon army that I control and destroy everything and everyone on this level."

"You forget yourself, Belial. You can't kill an Elysian like myself."

"Are you going to pretend you don't know about the blade you gave to their mother?"

Abaddon smirked. "I know of the blade I gave to her, but that doesn't mean it can kill me."

Belial paused, his gaze searching everyone on the other side of the table as though he could gauge the truth of Abaddon's words from them.

Her father slowly tapped his fingertips on the flat surface of the table. "You have nothing that would make me step down as ruler of the Underworld, and this little coup you're trying to pull off has failed before it's even begun."

Belial pushed to his feet, and a sharp pain sliced through Selena's middle. She sucked in a sharp breath as she fought the clawing sensation that radiated out from her stomach, carving its way up to her chest. Her breath was coming out in quick gasps, and her hands fisted on the tablecloth as sweat gathered on her forehead.

"Selena? What's wrong?" Though sitting right next to her, Raesean sounded like he was in a boat on the lake outside.

"Overconfidence is a family trait that seems to have skipped me." Evanora's voice floated over to her, and Selena cringed at both the pain blossoming in her chest and the manic smile on her sister's face. "Did you really think I couldn't break the spell you placed on the silly little mirrors in this house?"

Her sister curled her fingers into a ball as though she were wringing the last drop of juice from a zesty lemon. Selena's insides contracted, and the next thing she knew, she was looking up at the high ceilings in the dining room.

The heat in the room rose to match her boiling blood. Someone was shouting, which was followed by curses. Selena could follow none of it as she tried to fight back the pain.

A pair of almond-brown eyes and bright blue hair came into her vision. She blinked several times to get his face into focus.

"What can I do, Selena?" Shalik demanded. "Is it poison? Or magic?" He ran frantic hands over her body, searching for anything that might give him a clue as to what was happening to her.

"There's nothing you can do for her, blue boy." Evanora's heels clicked on the stone floor as she came closer. She stood looking down at Selena trembling on the floor, her body contorted in pain. "She used her blood to cast the spell on the mirrors, and now that I'm unraveling it, I'm ensuring she feels every single thread she's connected to."

Shalik placed his palms on each side of Selena's face to keep her gaze on him. "I don't know what she's doing, and my knowledge of mirror magic is limited, but I know your magic is much stronger than hers because I've seen you control every reflective surface in a room."

Another bout of pain sliced through Selena's body, and tears poured out of her eyes.

"Listen to me, Selena." Shalik was shaking her, trying to keep her in the here and now. "If you don't fight this, several demons are going to overrun the manor, and the only ones who have a chance of surviving are you and your dad."

His words sliced through all the pain she was feeling, reaching the fear she'd been burying over the last year. The fear of losing yet another person she cared about. Another member of her family slaughtered while she lay helpless to do anything.

Selena sucked in a jagged breath, searching deep in her well of magic she usually kept at bay. She didn't coax it forward like she normally would, maintaining control over it. No, she grabbed onto her power and dragged it to the surface with a scream.

Chapter 22

Everything had gone to shit.

Raesean stood frozen in the dark as Belial used his power to control darkness to cut him off from everything in the room. He could still hear Selena and Shalik on the floor close to where she'd collapsed, but the surrounding darkness was thick, and he didn't want to use his fire magic lest he set the wrong person aflame.

"You'll never win this." Abaddon's voice filtered into the thick darkness that trapped Raesean in place.

"But I already have," Belial taunted. Raesean could hear other voices—Evanora's and more of Shalik's. They were lower to the ground, which meant if he wielded his fire high enough and in the opposite direction, he could get himself out of this box.

Lifting his arms, he called the hottest flame to the palms of his hands and pressed them against the shadow box he was in.

He watched with satisfaction as the shadows fell in wisps to his feet.

Raesean glanced around the room to assess the situation. One demon lay with his eyes open and mouth frothing, probably from being hit with Abaddon's fear magic. Another demon lay dead on the floor, Cerberus sitting on his chest, eyeing Belial. Probably looking for a way to defend the ruler of the Underworld without destroying the dining room.

Belial had wrapped Abaddon in the same shadow magic he'd used on Raesean, knowing that the ruler wouldn't blindly send out his fear magic if it meant hitting the wrong person in the room.

The servants were gone, probably clearing the room the moment Selena had hit the floor, and Evanora was standing over Shalik as he held Selena's face in his hands.

Selena sucked in a breath, and the room fell silent. Like the calm before the storm, he could feel the pressure in the room build as the magic sparked and crackled in the air. Then the earth trembled, and all Raesean had time for was to throw himself to the floor before thousands of mirror shards came flying into the room.

They stood mid-air as though trained and waiting for a command from their master.

He crawled over to where Selena lay with her back arched off the ground. Her copper skin glowed like a flashlight reflecting off of a mirror, and her closed fists blazed bright with the white light of her magic. Raesean threw an arm up to shield his eyes.

"Selena," he shouted, but it might as well have been a whisper as her magic held her in its thrall. Her body levitated off the floor, inching upright until her toes pointed downward, and she faced her sister Evanora.

Selena's eyes were pools of mercury, and her brows lowered as she lifted her glowing fist. Then, the mirror shards moved, aiming for Evanora with unwavering accuracy.

Evanora tossed up her hand, calling on her own magic. The shards stopped inches away from her, trembling mid-air, fighting to move forward. Selena's brow dipped lower, and she gritted her teeth. The shards gained another few centimeters.

"End this now, Selena, or the demon army that your magic kept at bay will overrun us soon," Abaddon said from the other side of the room.

Raesean heard it then, the stomping of feet on hard-packed earth as they marched closer to the manor. Maybe Selena heard it too because she waved one hand to the left, sending shards of glass toward where Belial stood watching them.

"No!" Evanora screamed. Her concentration wavered as she struggled to fight an attack on two fronts. Some of the slivers of mirror that she'd been keeping at bay slipped through, impaling her sides and arms. Both the general and Evanora went down.

Selena inched forward until she was looking down on her sister, who crawled backward away from her.

"Your magic is powerful, and I understand why you think you can match me. But my magic is a little different. It grows whenever I use it, seeking power with every soul it sucks into a mirror, and I've sucked in a lot of souls since I returned to the Underworld. My magic wants to rule, and the only thing stopping it from taking control is the restriction I put on it."

Evanora lifted her chin, her eyes hard, even though she was bleeding out on the floor. "That's a lie. Everyone knows the test you took with the council last year rated you as a mid-level mirror witch."

Selena laughed, the sound shrill. Nothing like the warm, delighted sound she let out when she was really amused. "You really think I allowed that bitch Ofilia to know the actual level of my power? I knew she was up to something, so I avoided her as much as possible. What I should have done was eliminate her the moment she started threatening me. If I had, she wouldn't have teamed up with your stepdaddy's son to murder friends of mine. But don't you worry, I won't make the same mistake with you."

"Selena!" Abaddon's voice rang out across the room, stopping Selena from impaling her sister with more shards of glass. "Despite what she's done, she's still your sister."

She looked over her shoulder at her father, silent words passing between them before she pushed to her feet and backed away from the witch bleeding out on the floor.

Abaddon moved forward until he was looking down at his youngest daughter. "I don't know what life was like for you growing up, Evanora, but I'm giving you a chance to change the path you've taken. Leave the Underworld and never look back."

"I won't leave without Belial," she demanded.

"You can take his body with you," Abaddon whispered.

His words hit Evanora, and her body jerked as though struck by another round of glass. "Nooo," she wailed, grief blanketing the room. She struggled to her feet, rounding the table to where Belial lay on the floor, glass sticking out of him like toothpicks in cheese. Evanora's hate-filled eyes looked over at everyone in the room. "I promise you on his blood that I'll make you pay."

With the general of the demon army dead, the coup he tried to execute fizzled out like soda left out in the open for some days. Selena stuck around long enough to ensure Evanora vacated the premises, along with Belial's body. The mirror witch was still raging when Raesean dragged her out of the manor.

The demons who had been marching at the general's command tucked tail and ran after they saw his body. Raesean made an example of a few of them, turning them to ash.

Now Selena was sitting on the floor of her bedroom, her back to her bed, eyes unfocused, reliving the events of the evening.

Once again, she could have lost someone she cared about because she hadn't used the full potential of her magic.

Evanora should never have been able to break the spell she'd put on those mirrors, and she certainly should not have been able to use the breaking of the spell to inflict crippling pain on her. Even if she might have more knowledge of spellwork than Selena did.

A knock on the door had her looking up into Shalik's worried brown eyes.

"Hey," he said, walking into the room and lowering himself to the floor next to her. "You okay?"

She nodded, and Shalik scoffed. "Since when do you lie to me?"

The corner of her mouth tilted up, and he bumped his shoulder against hers. "Tell me what's wrong?"

"Other than the demons trying to kill my father, you, Raesean, and me? Not much."

He flipped his long blue hair to the other side of his shoulder and turned to face her. "You knew these things before the dinner, so I don't think that's the problem. Plus, you took care of the leader, so there won't be any attacks soon. So tell me, what's really bothering you?"

Selena huffed out a breath. There was very little she could get past Shalik. After all, they'd been living together for a year, and he was her brother in every way except blood. Maybe that was a good thing because her own blood sister just tried to kill her a few moments ago.

"I almost lost you again. You, my dad, Raesean, and maybe even Cerberus."

"Trust me, Cerberus would have changed and taken care of things if he thought the situation was that bad. That dog knows full well if we die, he won't get any more doggy treats, and he would not have that."

She burst out laughing, gripping her side as the laugh eased some of the worry that was plaguing her.

"He definitely would have leveled the manor for that," she said through sniffles and giggles. "Where is he, by the way?"

"He went with Raesean and your father to make sure there were no more demons on this level."

She nodded, her thoughts once again returning to how close she'd come to almost losing them all.

"Are you ready to tell me what's going on in that head of yours?"

"I keep thinking that if you weren't there to snap me out of the pain, would she have won? Would Evanora have killed all of us?"

Shalik reached and gripped her hand. "Don't do that, Lena. Thinking about what would have happened if you had done things differently is a surefire way to take you down a spiral you can't get out of."

She looked over at him, brows lowered, and a sheen covered his eyes. "After Mini died, I thought of so many things I could have done differently to save her. None of them brought her back. It only made me blame myself more and seek other ways to stop the pain."

Selena felt the usual pang in her chest whenever she thought about her best friend Mini and how she'd been brutalized to death by the demon Alden, Belial's nephew. Belial had gotten off easy with a quick death, his soul returned to the pit to be reborn again. Alden's soul, on the other hand, was Abaddon's new plaything and was probably begging to be extinguished.

"Every day I wake up, I wish I had never let Mini investigate the murders. If I had just let things go, she might still be alive."

"That's just the thing." Shalik squeezed her hand. "We could never have stopped Mini from doing anything she wanted. She was too headstrong for anything else, and when you found out about Ofilia and Alden, you quickly put a stop to them."

Selena shook her head, ready to make another argument about how she could have stopped them before they'd murdered her friend.

"No, Lena. I think what we're struggling with is the fact that there was nothing we could have done or said to save the ones we love, and we need to just let that go."

Her shoulders shook, and he pulled her into his arms, making small circles on her back. "We'll get through this," he whispered. "Just like we always do. Together."

She let out a sniffle of agreement. After a while, she untangled herself from him, wiping the tears from her eyes.

"Feel better?"

"Yes," she said with a breath, swiping her hand under her nose.

"And your magic?"

"It's fine."

"I thought we don't lie to each other?" He tilted his head as he gave her a hard look. "Your eyes are still silver, which means the magic is still running through you."

"They are?" She tried to stand, but Shalik held her firm.

"Tell me what's going on."

"My magic... I can feel it." She squirmed as her magic chose that moment to move, sliding through her like a hungry cat twining between her legs. "It's just under my skin fighting to be known, whispering dark demands to me..."

A shudder racked through her, and Shalik gripped her arms tighter. "You once told me that you pushed the strength of your magic down into a well so that no one could know its true level. Can you push it back into the well?"

Selena shook her head. "I tried, but I can't get it to lie dormant the way it used to."

"What do you mean?"

"Usually, when I want to use my magic, I call it to me, coax it up from the well until it fills me and I can use it. But this time, I forced it forward, and I think the well I used to keep it in cracked. Now my magic is continuously leaking out, and it has a mind of its own."

"Wasn't it always like that?"

"No... Before, it was in sync with me. It wanted what I wanted. If I was angry or sad, it matched my emotions. That all changed after I used it in the demonic ritual to capture Alden's soul. After that, it started making its own demands known. At first, I thought it was the pendant that was causing it and amplifying its thoughts, but now I think it's taken on a personality of its own."

"Is this new personality you have better than when Cerberus chews on your designer shoes?" Shalik asked with a small smile.

Selena let out a bitter laugh, just like he wanted her to. After a moment, she took a deep breath, then let it out slowly. Settling her back against the side of the bed, she shifted until her head was on his shoulder, and he slung an arm over her.

"I think my magic has a temper worse than when I'm angry at Cerberus. It wants to be recognized, acknowledged, and, more than anything, it wants power. I'm worried, Li. If I don't gain control of it one day, it will seek the power it wants."

"How does it gain the power it wants?"

She ran her tongue over her bottom lip. "How else would a mirror witch like myself gain power?"

"You don't mean..."

"My magic wants souls, and I'm currently in the one place that has a multitude of souls ready for the taking."

Chapter 23

*"T*he white demon would help us get the souls."*

Selena's eyes opened with a gasp. The voice in the darkness was soft, but she heard it as though it was...

"Yes."

Selena bolted upright in her bed, looking around the room, listening intently. Surely the voice wasn't coming from...

"Inside you."

"You're still glowing."

Her magic surged but didn't lash out, as though it knew who had spoken before she did.

"Jeez, Raesean, what are you doing skulking around in the dark?" She placed a hand over her racing heart as though she could slow it down to its usual rhythm. Raesean stood in the doorway to the bathroom with a towel draped around his waist, hair mussed. A sure sign he'd just run a towel through it.

"I wasn't skulking, just keeping an eye on you, and you're glowing."

Selena looked down at her copper skin and saw that he was right. There was a light sheen coming from her like a lantern with a dark shade turned down low. She wouldn't light up a room, but it was enough to let anyone looking at her know that her magic was active.

"I've never seen your magic do this before."

"That's because it's never done this before." She flopped back on the bed. Closing her eyes, she turned her focus inward to the magic, searching for the internal well where she usually stored her magic. The metaphysical lid that normally covered the well was crumbling, and her magic was leaking out more and more. "Shit."

"What's wrong?" She felt the mattress of the bed dip, and she could smell the faint smell of sulfur, ash, and the masculine scent that was uniquely him.

"I can't get my magic to lie dormant. When I forced it out against Evanora, I cracked the container I use to house it." There was a long silence, then the sheets rustled, and his alluring scent got stronger.

"How do you usually get it to lie dormant?" he whispered.

"There is a well inside of me. I normally store my magic in it, but the cover for the well is falling apart, and the walls of the well are cracking."

"Then don't put it back in the well." Warm fingers danced over one arm, then the other, leaving goosebumps in their wake.

"I can't just leave it to weave its way through me," Selena said, her voice breathy.

"I never said you should." His fingers danced over her throat now, and she angled her head sideways so that he had easier access to continue what he was doing. He let out a dark chuckle. His heated breath brushed over her face. He was closer now, much closer than she thought he was, and yet she still didn't open her eyes. "Instead of trying to fix the well, why don't you create something else to store it in?"

This time, Selena opened her eyes, and they locked on to his pale blue ones.

"I didn't say you could open your eyes."

His lips were a breath away from hers while his hands roamed over her exposed skin. After her talk with Shalik earlier about her magic and several failed attempts to get it back into its metaphysical well, she'd taken a shower and climbed into bed without a stitch of clothing on.

Now the demon was stretched out next to her, running his hands over the naked skin peeking out from under the light blanket she'd covered herself with. His hands slipped lower. Past her clavicle to the swells of her breasts, gently playing with the tops.

"Do you trust me?" he whispered. Selena paused, rolling the question around her mind. Could she trust a demon? She'd learned that demons were fickle, untrustworthy creatures who sought power by any means necessary. They thrived on chaos, making deals, and would double-cross you just for the fun of it. Trusting them is the last thing that anyone should do.

But Raesean. He wasn't just any demon. When Mini died, he'd tracked her down and found her wandering the streets in her grief. He'd tried to protect her from self-destructing when Lima and the other demons attacked her, and he made sure she made it to the Underworld. He'd stuck by her side through a lot. Never once trying to use her magic for gain.

Selena reached up and smoothed the hair he'd tousled after his shower. "Yes."

His eyes lit up for a split second before he gave her the most glorious smile. The hand that was trailing over her body made its way up to her face, where he ran a calloused thumb over her cheek.

"I want you to close your eyes again." Her eyes fluttered shut, and she breathed in the masculine musk of his skin so close to hers. "Inspect the well where you store your power. Feel the strength of the well. Why is it crumbling?"

She followed his instructions, looking deeper into herself at the crumbling stones that leaked her magic. She frowned.

"What's wrong?"

"The stones aren't strong enough to hold the magic anymore. My powers have increased."

"Yes, I've gotten stronger."

The voice had Selena jerking upright, eyes wide.

Raesean was quick to grab her arm, stopping her from bolting off the bed.

"What happened?"

"It… My magic. It spoke to me." Selena looked at him, a slight tremor racking through her body.

"And it's never done that before?"

She moved her head from side to side.

"Okay. I want you to lie back down." Gently, he pushed her backward until she was stretched out on the bed, eyes closed.

"Don't think about why your powers have increased. See if you can gauge how strong the magic is."

"It's strong, but I can still control it."

"Take a closer look at the power leaking out of the well. Touch it. Taste it." Raesean's words trailed over her skin, heating her blood and sending her heart racing. She rubbed her thighs together as the heat in her blood drifted south.

"Focus," he said with a dark chuckle.

"It's kinda hard with you breathing all over me," she muttered.

"If you can't concentrate while I'm doing the bare minimum, will you be able to contain and control your magic when you lose control of that explosive temper of yours? Poor Cerberus will run for the hills the moment he sinks his teeth into one of your shoes."

Selena scoffed. "What do you know about him and my shoes?"

"Trust me, I know a great many things about you."

"He deserves what he gets because he always targets the most expensive ones. Why doesn't he chew on some flip-flops? It's always the new ones."

"This entire conversation just proves my point." The sheets rustled, and the mattress sunk down on either side of her. She could feel the heat of his body hovering over hers, and his breath brushed against her lips moments before his words came out. "You need to pay attention to what you are doing while other things are happening. Otherwise, you're going to end up losing control of your magic, and I don't think you're ready to face the darkness growing in you."

"How do…"

"I can sense it. Felt it from the first day I saw you, but I didn't know what it was until I saw you use it on Alden in the pit."

Selena ran her tongue over her bottom lip, and she heard Raesean's breath catch. "Do you think I'm evil?"

His fingers roamed her body once more, and she fought the urge to open her eyes. A part of her wanted to see his face. To know for sure what he thought of her. Another part, the coward that she was, kept her eyes closed because she didn't want to see the rejection in his eyes.

"No one is completely good or evil." His soft, full lips pressed against her shoulder. "You just have to decide how much of each you want to be."

"What if my magic chooses for me?"

"Whatever you choose, I'll never leave your side. Now focus so you can get it under control and make your own choice."

She nodded, delving deep until she was once again looking within to her magic. More of it had leaked out and had taken on a spectral form.

"You'll never be able to contain me," it whispered with a taunting laugh.

"Can you feel its strength?" Raesean's voice reminded Selena what she needed to do. "Are you familiar with its sound, its smell, how it rebels against you?"

"Yes," she replied. She ran mental hands over the spectral form, familiarizing herself with the new facets of her magic.

"Now, think of a material that you believe can contain all that power."

Selena thought about titanium. A lightweight, tough material that has a small amount of flexibility to it but won't break. As she thought about the metal, a titanium disk mentally appeared in her hand.

"Do you have the material?"

"Yes."

"Use the material to construct a box over the well. Make it tall enough and wide enough so that it forms a barrier over and around the well. Not touching any of the sides."

"*No,*" the voice cried as though sensing its fate.

The spectral form it had conjured flew around her, trying to stop her from containing it. Selena ignored each brush of her magic as it fought against being trapped once more. She mentally produced more and more of the metal until she had the five parts of the box she needed to cover the well. Once that was done, she maneuvered them until the top and three sides were in place.

Selena turned to her magic, which was rushing around, trying to get her to stop. It couldn't, though, because it was her magic, not something corporeal until it left her body. She was in control, and she'd be damned if she let it rule her.

Shifting her focus, she grabbed the form by its arm, dragging it to the open side of the box. It screeched—a long, pitiful sound—as it tried to wrestle its escape with intangible hands that passed right through her. An effort in futility, as it was something that lived in her and had no way of stopping her.

"*Don't put me in the dark again. There is another way,*" it pleaded, attempting to dig its heels in.

"I'm sorry, but this is how it must be. It's too dangerous for me to give you free rein," Selena replied.

"*Please,*" it begged, "*not in the dark.*"

Selena tightened her hold on her thrashing magic, ready to shove it in, but then she paused. Her thoughts drifted to the demons from the pit who confronted her on her way to her father's manor. All they wanted was a chance to see the surface level. To step out of the dark they were born in so they could experience something new.

Maybe it was the demons or her magic's plea, but Selena conjured light. Thousands of fairy lights decorated the inner walls of the box and down the well, breaking up the inky black as far as the eyes could see.

Around the well, she grew blue and white wildflowers along with thick grass that you could sink your feet into or lay comfortably in while you looked at the light. Her magic ceased thrashing and stared at the lights and flowers in wonder.

"You did this for me?"

Selena nodded, walking her magic into the box.

"Why?"

"Because no matter who or what you are, no one deserves to be trapped alone in the dark."

She stepped out and quickly placed the last panel of the box in place with a quiet snick. She didn't hear any more screaming or fighting from her magic. Just a contented sigh and a calm she hadn't felt in a long time.

Chapter 24

"**Y**ou're not glowing anymore."

Raesean hovered over her, waiting for her eyes to flutter open so he could ensure they were back to their usual brown and not the mirrored mercury that bleeds over them when she is at the height of her power.

He waited one heartbeat, then two before her thick lashes lifted with her lids, and he was looking down into the eyes that had been haunting him since the moment he spotted her in his club.

"There you are," he whispered. His lips were a breath from hers, and he lay there waiting. Just like he did all those years ago when she'd adamantly stated she would never date a demon. Back then, he'd thought it was the stigma that all demons were untrustworthy.

It was only a year ago he'd discovered she'd done it because she hadn't wanted any demon to find out who her father was. If they had, they definitely would have used her to get the throne. Demons seek power; it was in their nature, but he'd never wanted power taken from others. He preferred to amass his own power, which he did. So he hadn't wanted her for her power.

He'd just wanted her.

Unfortunately, when he'd discovered who her father was, he'd thought she was making her own bid for the throne, and he'd pushed her away. She'd never forgiven him for that. Now she was lying under him with nothing between them except the light sheet that was hanging on to her pointed nipples by sheer will.

She reached a hand up and pushed a lock of his hair from his face, and he was done waiting. He crashed his lips against hers, savoring the way her breath caught. She tasted like a mix of cream and the sweetest cherries, and he wanted to swallow her whole.

Pulling away, he trailed his lips over her cheeks, jaw, and down her neck where his fingers had caressed her earlier. Her body responded just like before, heating under his lips, goosebumps pebbling on her skin.

"I'd been a fool to walk away from you a year ago," he whispered while his tongue did wicked things that made her moan.

"It's fine," she gasped. "I'll forgive you if you keep doing whatever you're doing now."

He smirked against her copper skin, relishing how her stomach muscles tightened when his breath hit her.

"Trust me. I plan to earn your forgiveness and more."

He trailed his lips lower until he buried his face between the two mounds he'd teased the tops of moments ago. They were a handful. Enough that he could bring them together and kiss each side without moving his head, but he did anyway because why not?

Selena writhed under him while simultaneously running her hands over any part of him she could reach. His shoulders, his sides, even running her hands through his hair.

Raesean rubbed his cheek against a pebbled nipple, drawing the dark nub into his mouth to swirl his tongue around the hard flesh.

"Oh," she groaned.

He spent some time alternating between one breast and the next, noting every time she mewled, cursed, and thrashed under him. Her pleasure was his to learn, to give, and he soaked up the knowledge like a youngling learning something for the first time.

"Rae," she begged. He wasn't sure what she was begging for, but the sound of it got his cock harder than rock, and he was going to find out exactly what she wanted.

Releasing his two prizes, he pushed back until he was kneeling over her. He pulled off the rest of the light sheet she'd covered herself with so that he could see the rest of her body.

The same one that had been driving him crazy with every sway of her hips and shake of her ass as she walked away from him.

Last year was the closest he'd come to having his hands on her, and they'd been interrupted. He still hadn't forgiven the damn dog for that. This time, though, every demon in the Underworld could knock on the door, and he wouldn't be able to stop himself.

Maybe he'd been staring at her for too long because she moved to cover herself.

"Don't," he commanded, wrapping his hand around her wrist. "Let me see what I'll be feasting on for the rest of the night."

She nibbled on her lower lip and then relaxed. He could practically see the confidence she usually waved like a red flag in front of him slipping back into place. To say he was shocked she wasn't secure in the magnificence of her body was an understatement.

Tonight, he would make it his mission to let her know he delighted in every aspect of her, every curve, beauty mark, and line on her body. It was his privilege to be with her, and he would take all night to show her.

"You have me at a disadvantage here," she muttered while he traced his hand over the smooth skin of her stomach to the sunken area of her hips.

"How so?" He dipped his hands into the V between her thighs, running a finger over the bundle of nerves at the top.

"Shit," she cursed, squeezing her eyes shut. "You have me completely naked, yet you're still covered."

She slid her hand over his chest, dipping her fingers into the ridges of his stomach, the top of the towel still tightly wrapped around his waist. She gave it a little tug, and it unraveled much like she was the more he touched her body.

Raesean skimmed the fingers he had on her clit lower until he reached her warm, wet entrance, sliding two of them in. She was dripping.

"Fuck," he swore when he felt how much she'd enjoyed what he had been doing to her. He removed his hand, slipping the fingers through his lips. His eyes rolled back into his head at her delectable taste. All sweet and tart. He was never a dessert person, but he would make an exception for her.

He needed to feast now.

Shifting so that he was in front of her splayed open before him, he lowered himself before his goal, sliding his hands up her inner thigh, following his hands with kisses until he was at her apex. He pushed a finger inside, taking pleasure in the way her body sucked him in, gripping him tight, spilling more of her hot liquid over his fingers and hand.

He could only imagine how fantastic she was going to feel when he finally forced his cock into her, but he could wait. First, the feast. He lowered his face, inhaling her sweet scent. It was like a drug that loosened his muscles and hardened his cock even more than he thought possible.

Raesean pushed her thighs wider, slipping his hand under her to lift her up to his mouth like a chalice to a king, gripping her thick globes to ensure she didn't move. Then he ran his tongue from entrance to clit, fighting to keep things slow as she jerked in his hands.

"Nuh-uh. Don't take away my new treat, Lena. You won't like the consequences."

"I wouldn't..." she gasped out when he ran his tongue over her again, "dream of it."

"Just remember that."

Then he dove in. Alternating between licking up every drop of her juices to sucking on her clit to produce more. He had a self-reproducing treat, and if he drowned in the taste of her, he was going to return to Amaryllis a happy demon.

Her thighs quivered, and she sunk her hands into his hair, gripping for purchase as she pushed her core into his face, seeking that little extra that would send her over the edge. He was happy to oblige, balancing with one hand before sinking a finger into her center, rotating it until he felt that raised spot inside. Then he pressed, sucking her clit at the same time.

She detonated.

Raesean looked down the length of her body as she writhed, screaming her pleasure, amping up his own. He licked up every drop he had wrung out of her, knowing he'd become thoroughly addicted to her taste, and he was okay with that.

The soft palms that had been pulling his hair out at the roots were now pushing his shoulders to get him to stop. It was only because he wanted to taste other parts of her that he gave her a reprieve.

Her breath sawed in and out as he moved his lips over her body. He licked and nipped her hips, gliding his hands up to her breasts to lightly pinch her nipples.

Whimpering, she gripped his hands before he could do more.

She sat up, shoving his shoulders so that he fell back on the bed. She rained kisses over his face, peppering his eyes, nose, and chin with her soft, full lips. It was almost like she was thanking him for giving her pleasure. She needn't have bothered. He would do it again in a heartbeat.

Her kisses moved lower to his neck, where she gently bit him before continuing down. When she got to his abs, she ran her tongue over every indentation. Raesean's blood heated the more she touched him, teased him, and he was ready to wring another orgasm out of her.

Her hands brushed the length of his cock, and it bounced up in response. Just when he was getting ready to flip her over, her mouth enveloped him, and he was sliding down the back of her throat without so much as a breath of warning.

"Fucking Abyss," he shouted. Pleasure leaped up his spine as she hollowed her cheeks, bobbing her head so that he slid in and out of her wicked mouth.

His hands fisted the sheets as he fought not to grip her hair and fuck her mouth like he wanted to. Selena hummed as though she heard his thoughts, the sound heightening his pleasure, and he swore again. She glided him out of her until all that remained in her mouth was the tip. She then swirled her tongue around the sensitive head, lapping at the pre-cum like her favorite ice cream, before sliding him back down her throat, proving she had no gag reflex.

Unintelligible noises escaped him as she worked him over with her tongue, teeth, and hands, caressing his balls with delicate fingers while she destroyed him with her mouth.

Sweat beaded on his brow, and he felt the telltale tingle move up his spine. His hand gripped the sheets, and he fought the magnetic pull of release.

"Selena," he warned. "I'm close."

But instead of releasing, she worked him faster as though she wanted to suck his soul out of the tip, the way she would with her mirrors. Selena hollowed her cheeks, letting out a low hum before running her fingers once more over his balls. Then she shifted her gaze so that she was looking directly into his eyes. All of her desire showed out, and it was the most beautiful thing he'd ever seen.

That was it. That was his undoing as his muscles contracted, and he released himself with a loud roar.

Raesean watched with rapt attention as Selena gave one last pleasure-inducing pull before releasing him with a pop. She ran a tongue over her lips with a satisfied smirk while he fought to catch the breath he'd lost when she'd undone him.

"That was…" Words failed him.

"Delightful?" She kissed up his body, rubbing her hard ripples against his abs, then chest, until her lips were a hair's breadth away from his. "Amazing?"

Raesean reached up and grabbed each globe of her ass and forced her down until she was sitting on his rebounding cock. "Fucking mind-blowing."

She chuckled, and an emotion he couldn't quite identify shifted in him. He took her lips. Gently this time.

He poured everything he felt into the kiss. Every emotion he couldn't name. Her hands gripped the sheets as though she was seeking purchase for the onslaught of feeling from him.

She pulled away, lids heavy but eyes wary as she looked at him.

"It's okay," he whispered, knowing she was fighting against what she was feeling. "I've waited years for you, and I'll wait for you until the end. Tell me when you're ready."

He took her lips before she could deny the truth of what was between them. She was a stubborn one, and if forced to acknowledge her feelings before she was ready, she would run for the hills. After what had happened tonight, he didn't have time to track her down and drag her back to where she belonged.

So he deepened the kiss, turning it from something gentle to something more demanding, physical, so that she could hide behind that shield for the moment. His hands roamed her body, roving over sweat-slicked skin, and he gloried in the keening sound she made, like a worshipper being acknowledged by a goddess. His goddess, and he would worship at her altar for all of eternity if she would let him.

"Rae, please."

Her words obliterated the last thread of control he had. He twisted so that she was under him, shoving her thighs apart as he pushed her knees to her chest, and her ass rose an inch off the bed. The perfect angle to enter her with one forceful stroke. She cried out, her nails raking over his arms as she fought against the pleasure that assaulted her.

Her inner walls fluttered against his hard cock, and he swirled his hips, letting out his own groan of pleasure when she tried to strangle his dick.

"Your pussy likes that, doesn't she?" he muttered, retreating and slamming into her again. "She likes it when I fuck her hard."

Her thick juices were painting him, leaking out with every slam of his hips. He was almost tempted to eat her out again, but it would take all the angels from Elysium to get him to leave the tight heat of her body.

"More," she begged, lifting her hips to meet his as he powered back and forth.

"As my lady commands."

Shifting his knees, he angled his body, then pistoned into her, their flesh slapping against each other, their grunts and screams of pleasure echoing off the room's walls. Her sheath clamped down on him like a vice, and she let out a silent scream as her back arched off the bed. Raesean reached down and pinched her nipples, all the while keeping up the punishing pace he'd set.

The pleasure on her nipples caused her to grip him even tighter, amping up his rapture. His cock swelled, and he rode the wave of her pleasure until he found his own, emptying everything he had into her.

Chapter 25

Selena stepped out of her room with a bounce in her step, fighting a big grin from taking over her face. Her magic was under control, and she'd just had the best sex of her life, and she wasn't exaggerating in the least.

And though she would never admit this because his ego didn't need stroking, the demon ruined her for anyone else. There was no way any being on the surface world or in the Abyss would be able to do that.

"Good morning."

Shalik's voice had her looking over her shoulder. He'd just stepped out of his room, pin-straight blue hair hanging to one side to show the shaved side of his head. He wore a fitted black T-shirt and jeans, and his sneaker footfalls were silent on the carpeted hallway, with Cerberus quick on his heels.

"Morning," she responded cheerily.

Shalik gave her his signature devious smile that warned her she wouldn't like what he was about to say.

"I would ask if you slept well, but from the screams coming from your room into the wee hours of the morning, I don't think you got much sleep last night."

Selena shoulder-checked him, which was more shoulder to arm, before continuing down the hall. "I'll have you know I slept very well last night."

"Yeah, because you probably slipped into a coma after round three."

"Oh my god." She felt the blush creep up her cheeks. Thank goodness her copper skin wouldn't show it.

"You said that a few times this morning too."

Selena backhanded him in the stomach, and he laughed at her. Her heart swelled at his good-natured ribbing. It meant that he was finally getting past his grief of losing Mini, and it gave her hope that she would eventually get past her own guilt and rage for her friend's murder.

Cerberus let out a sharp bark, racing ahead to the dining room where a late breakfast was being served. The incorrigible little mutt probably smelled his favorite treats. Selena walked into the dining room and stutter-stepped, not expecting the demon she spent hours being pleasured by to be sitting at the table with her father.

The pair looked up at her, and her stomach shifted, like someone had released a batch of tiny pixies, and they were fluttering inside of her. When she'd woken this morning with him gone, she'd been relieved. She needed to process what had happened the night before and what it meant.

Now, a slow smirk was climbing up his face as he watched her squirming in her flats. Raesean stood, inching his way to her, one hand in his crisp suit pants pocket. He stood looking down at her for a heartbeat before he tilted her chin up, leaned down, and placed a sweet kiss on her lips.

"Good morning," he whispered when he pulled away. "I hope you didn't think this... thing between us was going to be a secret."

Selena shook her head, even though the thought had crossed her mind briefly when she'd woken and found him gone.

He arched a brow at her as if to say he didn't believe her. She gave him an innocent smile. Raesean leaned forward to whisper in her ear. "In case I never mentioned it, I want everyone to know whom you belong to so they know that their death would be slow and painful, and my eyes would be the last thing they see before they're sent to their appropriate level in the Abyss."

Selena swallowed at the intensity in his eyes.

Shalik let out a snicker behind her, pushing past the pair. "Elysium help anyone who gets between the two of you. A fire demon and a mirror witch with a bad temper."

Raesean shrugged at Shalik's words before ushering her to her seat next to Abaddon.

Her father was slicing through his French toast, unconcerned that his right-hand man and his heir were involved. She had to admit that one reason she'd thought to keep quiet about what happened was her father's reaction. She should have trusted his ability to handle any situation, probably an ability developed over the centuries he'd been alive.

"Hello, Father." Selena piled her plate with scrambled eggs, bacon, and toast.

"Don't think, because you've got him to defend you, that means you can get away from eating your vegetables." Abaddon pointed his syrup-covered knife at the pitcher surrounded by some shot glasses. "Shalik was kind enough to help the cook with a recipe that included the right amount of nutrients you need down here."

"Did he now?" Selena shot her best friend a look of death while he calmly poured her a concentrated shot.

"I promise you won't taste the vegetables in there. Only the juice." He handed her the glass. She rolled her eyes at him before taking the glass and knocking back its contents.

"I'm surrounded by bossy men. If Mini were here, she would have already told you guys off."

The pain was a lance in her chest. For a moment, she'd forgotten that her friend, her sister, was gone and would never be a part of this new dynamic of her life.

Abaddon laid down his cutlery. "I'm sorry about what happened to Mini."

Selena nodded.

"I hope you find some comfort that Alden is still suffering the consequences of what he did."

She let out a soft breath, using her fork to dance the eggs around her plate, and her father cleared his throat.

"Now that we've dealt with the demon mutiny, I wanted to talk to you about your position as my heir to the throne of the Underworld."

She looked up at him, waiting for him to go on.

"When you initially left, you didn't want to be heir to the throne. As I mentioned, you weren't born in Elysium, so you don't have the restrictions I do. You can balance things so the Underworld caters to all souls. Change things so that all souls have an afterlife."

Selena chewed on her bottom lip, turning his words over in her mind. "What will happen if I included souls that aren't accepted into Elysium? Some of them would go to the Lucien level. What then? Would the angels take them to Elysium?"

Abaddon shrugged. "Change the rules and see."

"I'll think about it," she said, shoving a strip of bacon into her mouth.

Her father shifted in his seat as though he wasn't comfortable with what he had to say next. "I hope you're thinking about sticking around down here for a bit. I don't believe you have anything on the surface that needs your presence."

"Uh..." Selena said around her mouthful.

"I mean, if you return to the surface, who knows when you'll be back down here."

"Oh yeah. Shalik and I aren't in a hurry to head topside. As you know, things have been crazy, and, well, this has been a nice getaway for us, you know."

"Sure, sure."

"So we plan to stick around a while. And even if we were to go back, we would have to come back every so often because Shalik is going to need to get his hands on those vegetables for his potions. We can't get them on the surface."

Selena gave her father a small reassuring smile, and he reached a hand out to grip hers, which was subconsciously tracing patterns on the tabletop.

"Good, good." Abaddon stood, straightening his suit jacket. "When you're finished with breakfast, we can take a tour of the other levels to make sure everything is back to rights. It would be good for you to see what's changed over the years."

"Okay. I'll meet you outside in thirty minutes."

With a nod of his head, Abaddon left the dining room. Selena turned back to her food, swallowing the lump in her throat.

"I hope you know I will hold you to those trips for the vegetables," Shalik said. His knife screeched gently against his plate as he cut into his toast.

Selena rolled her eyes at him, but she couldn't help but smile. Her life had done a one-eighty in a matter of hours. Her magic was back under control, her sister and Belial's plan to replace her father was foiled, she was building something with Raesean, and all the people she cared about were safe.

After the year she'd had, she wouldn't question it. She couldn't afford to jinx her good luck.

Selena kicked off her sneakers, stripping off her clothes on her way to the shower. The trip to the demon level had taken more energy than she'd thought it would. It had been an emotional roller coaster of epic proportions.

First, seeing all the angry demons who wanted her and her father dead had stirred her magic, making her surly. She nipped their displeasure in the bud after she'd sucked out the soul of the first demon who had confronted her. When the others had seen her place it in a mirror and give it to her father, they'd all grown silent.

Fortunately, her magic had settled after her demonstrations as though satisfied to return to its fairy-lit home. Raesean had smirked at the demonstration, whispering in her ear.

"Vicious creature."

Then, he and her father had worked through the ranks of the demons in the army to select a new general.

Selena stepped under the hot spray of the shower, thinking about the next stop the three of them had made. Unlike the demon army, who spent most of their time either training or in bars, the housing area for demons who weren't soldiers was the complete opposite.

In the surface world, beings only saw demons as deal-making, power-hungry creatures, but on the demon level, they formed families. Young ones played in the park and fought each other over silly slights. There was even a school where they learned how to use their magic.

They lived under the scarce light of twilight, with lamps, torches, and fireplaces to aid in any darker areas. The demon level didn't have the faux sunshine Abaddon had on his level, and Selena could understand why so many of them wanted to go to the surface.

Maybe she could get a witch to cast the same spell her mother had done on Abaddon's level when she became queen. She paused at the thought. Did she now want to rule the Underworld?

Grabbing her towel, she pushed the thought away and dried off, quickly getting dressed to hunt Shalik down. He'd opted not to go on the tour, stating he'd prefer to wander through her father's garden, then take another nap as someone's pleasure screams had kept him awake until morning.

His comment had earned him a punch in the side, but she left him to his own devices. Stepping out into the hallway, she took the few steps to his door, then knocked. She waited a beat before knocking again.

When there was no response, she gripped the brass knob and twisted, pushing the silent door open. The bed was rumpled, but Shalik wasn't in it.

A niggling feeling wormed its way around the base of her spin like an icy finger against her skin.

Maybe he's in the garden.

She hurried out of his room, her quick steps taking her down the hallway and out the wooden front doors. She followed the path to her father's garden, eyes darting around the green-marked area.

"Shalik," she called out. Silence greeted her. She continued making her way to the back of the manor where the lake was. The boat she normally took out on the water was still there, so he couldn't possibly be out on the lake.

She turned away, outright running back into the house. Maybe he'd been waylaid by her father. They could be in his office right now, scheming new ways to get her to eat more vegetables.

Her feet slapped against the ground as she raced to her father's office, throwing open the door. It slammed against the wall with a thud.

Her father looked up at her from behind his desk, and Raesean, who was sitting in the visitor's chair, got to his feet.

"What's wrong?" he demanded.

"Have you guys seen Shalik? I can't find him. He's not in any of his usual places."

"I'm sure he's somewhere about cooking up more potions. We'll find him. Cerberus," her father called out.

The sleeping mutt, she hadn't noticed in her panic, opened tired eyes and glared at her father.

"Don't give me that look," her father muttered. "Find Shalik."

The dog gave a sharp bark, then scuttled out the door, his tiny paws padding on the floor, butt wiggling in his wake. Everyone quickly followed.

Selena's heart was racing, and it wasn't from all the running she'd been doing. The icy feeling she'd felt earlier was making its way toward her heart, fisting it in its grip.

They got to Shalik's bedroom, and Cerberus darted in, heading straight for the bathroom, where he paused before letting out a loud growl. The sight before her had her racing heart stopping.

It was like a movie playing over the mirror in the bathroom. In it was a bound and gagged Shalik on his knees, eyes wide as he looked up at Evanora. Shards of mirror were hovering over her hand, and she was manipulating them the way a juggler would roll balls in their hands. In her other hand was a strange blade that she waved back and forth as though saying no.

The image dimmed, and then the mirror fogged up before turning into a silver pool. A slip of paper floated to the surface, and Selena reached in and snatched it out.

"You took someone important to me. It was only fair I did the same. You can have him back. Just hand our father over, and you can have your precious brother."

The paper crumpled in her fist, and fissures appeared in the mirror before her, the tinkling sound of breaking glass echoing around the tiny bathroom. The pieces of the mirror came loose, falling to the ground with a loud crash, along with the pieces of her heart.

Chapter 26

"We'll get him back," Abaddon whispered to her.

Selena was sitting in her father's office, keeping a tight leash on her temper and her magic. She wanted to go down to the demon level and destroy every single demon until she had her best friend, her brother, her family by her side.

Evanora thought she'd seen the worst of Selena's magic last night, but she had no idea that for years, Selena had been fighting to temper off her magic so that she didn't bring attention to herself.

Now that she was in the Underworld, there was no reason to hide, to keep her magic in check. She and her magic agreed that they would rip the seven levels of the Underworld apart to get Shalik back, and she had a well of magic to do so.

"Selena?"

Raesean's voice pulled her attention back to the discussion they were having about how to get Shalik back.

"We need to find out where Evanora is keeping him. Once we do, we can sneak in and get him out safely. Then we can deal with Evanora and any other demons working with her." Abaddon looked over a map of the demon level, noting areas Evanora could remain unseen in.

"There aren't many places where she could hide him. Many of the younger demons don't associate with the soldiers, as you saw today," Raesean said with a glance at Selena. "They prefer to live a normal life as much as possible. Chances are, the demons who are helping her were in Belial's inner circle, and that means they would be somewhere they usually meet up."

Their words rolled over her as her focus pinged between keeping her magic in check and thoughts about storming the demon level. She wanted to slice them all into ribbons.

"Selena."

She blinked, and her gaze locked with Raesean's. He was kneeling in front of her, his hands clasping hers. "Are you okay?"

"Yes." The one syllable came out as a croak like she'd been screaming for hours. Like her inner screams were manifesting in her physical body.

Was that possible?

"It's okay if you can't do this. We'll get him back for you."

Her body jerked like he'd slapped her. "I won't sit by waiting for someone else to save him. I should have protected him, and since I failed at that, I have to be the one to get him back."

"Then I need you to pull yourself together because I won't save him if it means losing you."

The pair of them stared at each other for a heartbeat, with unspoken words thrown to the floor like a gauntlet. He wouldn't let her go near Evanora if he thought she couldn't handle herself. Little did he know she was more than ready to prove that she could get rid of her sister once and for all.

"We should question a few of the soldiers to gather more information on what Evanora's doing. It might limit the number of places we'd have to search."

Abaddon's voice broke the silent argument between Raesean and Selena.

"Wait. You're going?" Selena looked at her father.

"Of course I bloody am."

"You can't," Selena insisted. "She wants you there. She plans to use the blade on you. If you're stabbed with it, then she gets exactly what she wants. You. Out of her way."

"I've thought about that, and even if she wanted to kill me, she can't." Abaddon laid a hand on her shoulder.

"But she could send you into a hundred-year sleep, which is just as bad." Selena reached up and gripped his fingers.

"Raesean, could you give me a moment with my daughter?"

Silent as the night, the demon exited the office, leaving Selena alone with her father.

He took the seat next to her, wrapping both of his hands around hers.

"I know my methods as a father may not have been to your liking, but I did the best I could." The corners of his lips jerked up in a tight smile. "I've been alive for centuries, and the thought of having a child never occurred to me. Then I met your mother, and it was like everything was different. I immediately petitioned to have her as mine, and they denied me. So I broke the law of angels mating with non-angels without permission, and I'll never regret it because I had you. That's how important you are to me. I broke the law I valued more than anything to be with your mother and to have you, Selena, and was banned from Elysium because of it. Never forget that. And don't be afraid to carve your own path, no matter what anyone else says."

Selena wrapped her arms around her father, squeezing him close. "Don't let her take you away from me," she mumbled into his shoulder.

"I won't," he muttered.

He stood, walking around his desk to pull out the box he'd placed in there when she'd first arrived. Grabbing a letter opener from his desk, he pressed it to his index finger. Blood welled to the surface, and he touched it to the box, unsealing its contents.

He pushed back the lid, lifting her necklace with the red mirrored pendant out of it.

"I think, under the circumstances, you should have this back. We don't know what we're going to face when dealing with Evanora, and I'd rather you lose control of your magic than fall into her hands." He let out a little scoff. "Though I know with the level of magic you showed last night, I shouldn't be worried."

Though he meant the words as a comfort, Selena couldn't help but feel a sense of dread. Her entire family would be on the demon level, and the only thing that would ensure they walked out of there was the strength of her magic.

Raesean always hated the demon level.

It was dark, disgusting, disquieting, and a whole lot of alliterations he could use that showed his hatred for this place. There might be areas that were well-kept and housed families, but when he was on the streets, it was eat or die. He'd been a scrawny thing back then. No demon had wanted to take him under their wing because he'd had no power for the longest while. He'd had to cheat, steal, and lie his way into a full meal, and even then, some days he went hungry.

His powers had come much later than most demons, and when they did, he couldn't control them. They had been too much, and it was all he could do to prevent them from converting everything around him into ash. He'd been lucky Abaddon had taken him in when he did; otherwise, he doubted he would have been alive to see his first fifty years, let alone his first hundred.

Now he was back down here, in the piss and grime, slinking through pitch-black alleyways leading the being who saved him, and his daughter he loved, to what could possibly be their deaths. To say he wasn't happy about it was an understatement.

The plan they'd come up with was warm or half-baked at best. The three of them would do the scouting themselves, starting with the bar where most of the soldiers partied. Once they found Shalik, they would then decide on the next steps to save the potion master. Raesean had volunteered to go alone, but the pair of them had quickly vetoed that idea.

If he'd had his way, he would have just leveled everything to the ground. Then again, that wouldn't have been a good idea for the potion master, considering they didn't know exactly where he was. It would have also killed any innocent demons just trying to survive.

Something scurried in the dark, and it sounded more like it had two legs than four. Raesean halted, using the scant light from windows and doorways to search the darkness for any sign that they were being watched or of an imminent attack.

Silence pressed in on him, and it made Raesean more antsy. Something wasn't right, and just like in the darkness, he couldn't see things clearly enough to tell what was wrong.

First, the scout hadn't returned with information about Sha-lik's whereabouts. Then, when they'd opted to come down here just the three of them, the path had been suspiciously clear. Where were the drunken demons making deals or playing cards? Where were the smokers who hung out in the alleys waiting for an easy target to take advantage of? It was like everyone had cleared out because they knew trouble was coming.

Which brought him to the third problem he was having. It was silent. There was no one wailing in pain. No brash laughter or the sound of flesh hitting flesh as demons fought over scraps in the street.

This was a trap.

He turned to Selena and Abaddon, hoping to convince them that they should turn back when the alley lit up like kindling doused in gasoline. Someone had blocked off the furthest end of the alley with flames almost as hot as the hell fire he wielded. The other end had demons marching toward them.

Abaddon stepped around him, giving his hand a careless wave, whispering to the demons. "Tell me, what do you fear?"

No sooner had the words slipped past his lips than the demons fell to their knees screaming, in pain or, more likely, fear. Abaddon had wielded his power to inflict fear in others. The poor fools were probably seeing their own nightmares playing out before their eyes.

Raesean shook his head in disgust. It was obvious Evano-ra sent the younger demons to capture them. Older demons would know that if you stepped out of line, you could be tortured if you were alive. It's only the dead ones who were out of Abaddon's torturous reach because their souls return to Amaryllis to be reborn.

Abaddon continued out of the alley, stepping over the demons writhing in pain like left-out trash. "I don't think we need to sneak around anymore. Raesean, light the way."

Raesean conjured a fireball floating out in front of them. What he saw next had him wanting to grab Selena and drag her back to her father's manor, where she had some semblance of safety.

Hundreds of demons stood in formation on the street, waiting patiently for their leader to give the command. Belial gone, they'd thought the army would follow the command of the new general. They'd thought wrong. The new general lay with his throat ripped out in a pool of his own blood. Someone had beaten his body so badly that bones and tissue were poking out of various parts of his skin.

Shalik kneeled next to the broken body, his mouth tied with a strip of white cloth to gag him. His hands were bound behind his back, and his eyes widened when he looked over at Selena.

Delicate hands rested on his shoulders before they tightened, causing Shalik to scream behind the gag. Selena surged forward, and Raesean gripped her arm before she could do something that caused Shalik's death.

"I knew you'd come, Selena, but I had my doubts whether you'd bring our father."

Evanora stepped away from Shalik, her heeled boots splashing in the general's blood.

"Well, I'm just happy you could make it on such short notice. How do you like my army?"

Chapter 27

Selena was tired of hearing her sister's voice.

"Soldiers, please escort our guest to the bar where refreshments are waiting. We're going to have a nice, quiet family reunion."

There she was again, enjoying the sound of her own voice. To Selena, it was like nails on glass, a great feat considering she was a mirror witch.

The gloating tone she used was just short of making Selena want to cut her tongue out. In fact, the only reason she hadn't done that yet was because her little demon minions kept Shalik surrounded with a blade to his throat.

Selena searched the area for any weakness as the demons corralled her father, Raesean, and herself to the bar on the demon level, where the members of Belial's demon army hung out. According to Evanora, it was her army now, and Selena supposed since they were following her to their deaths, then her sister would be correct.

Abaddon overlooked their previous transgressions because he believed they were only following their general. They were soldiers trained to follow orders. Now, though, with the newly appointed general's blood seeping into the cracks in the street, Abaddon would wipe them out for their choice.

Selena would gladly help him reduce the army's numbers.

"I'd hold off on that thought for now," Raesean warned, accurately guessing the direction her thoughts had gone.

"Trust me, I am," she muttered.

The doors to the bar swung open, and Selena stepped into the large, brightly lit room. She pushed back the hood of her black hoodie, and her curls sprung free as she scanned the scene in front of her.

Demons covered the area. Females were walking around with drinks on wooden trays dressed in short leather pants that did nothing to cover the curves of their butts. Maybe that was the point, as the drinkers would grab a cheek, then a drink as they passed by.

The sound of fists hitting flesh had Selena turning her head in time to see a brawl break out between two demons. One of them was pummeling the other onto the floor. Blood flew from the mouth and nose of the demon on the floor, and the crowd cheered, while she wrinkled her nose in disgust.

Every table and chair on the floor was covered in blood, spit, or alcohol, and Selena wanted to call in a hazmat team to quarantine and fumigate the area. Her sneakers made a suction sound as she moved between the demons, forcing them forward.

Selena fought back a gag.

"Isn't this marvelous?" Evanora's red-heeled boots tapped on the travertine floor. She playfully bumped Selena with her leather-clad hip as she sauntered by with a wink. Selena wanted to impale her in the eye.

Evanora threw her hands wide. "Look at what freedom looks like."

She gave a slow turn as her crop top rode high. She pitched her voice over the clamoring in the bar. "We can do what we want when we want. No one can stop us. We're stronger, have more magic, and there is nothing that can stop us from taking what we want."

"Freedom seems more like a cesspool," Abaddon murmured as he moved to Selena's side. He wrinkled his nose as he glanced around the room. "Don't even get me started on how their destructive behavior is being rewarded. The complete opposite reason for the creation of the Underworld."

"That's exactly my point." Evanora sauntered over, her hips swaying with every step. She patted Abaddon on his chest. "We're tired of having to live in the shadows and obey your rules, Abaddon. I think it's time you let someone else take the throne."

Abaddon brushed her hand off the lapel of his suit. "Someone like you? I don't think so. You wouldn't even know the first thing about what it takes to keep order in the Underworld. You can't even keep this bar intact."

Evanora's eyes flared. "The bar is fine, and every soldier here is getting a taste of the freedom they've wanted for years."

"Yes, the freedom to take a piss in a place where the toilet is five steps away." Abaddon pointed a finger to match the judgmental tone in his voice. Evanora whipped her head around to follow the direction he was pointing.

In the far corner of the bar, a demon had whipped out his member and sprayed the side of the wall with urine.

"Hey," Evanora snapped at the demon. He looked over in a drunken haze. "Do that in the bathroom, or at the very least, outside."

The demon shrugged, stuffed his still-leaking member back in his pants, and shuffled to the bathroom.

"Not so easy to control a bunch of beings when you promise them unlimited freedom, is it?"

"I guess that's not something you'll have to worry about for much longer." Selena's sister looked past them to the demons holding Shalik. "Bring him forward."

Two of the demons brought a struggling Shalik forward, forcing him back to his knees before her, still keeping the blade to his throat. Evanora walked around the bar, where she reached under and pulled out a slim red box with gold hinges on the side.

Gently, she laid the box on the sticky bar top. Grasping the lid, Evanora lifted it, the hinges squeaking from disuse. She turned the box around so that it faced them.

Selena let her eyes rove over the slim white blade, nestled in the satin fabric lining the inside of the box. For something that could send her father into a sleep for a hundred years, it was a bit ordinary. It was about eight inches long and two inches wide.

Unlike other blades, it was white, made from a material that probably didn't exist on either the surface world or in the Underworld. One end of it tapered off to half the width of the blade and was wrapped with a strip of black material she couldn't identify.

"Beautiful, isn't it?" Evanora took the blade from the box, balancing it in her palm. "The craftsmanship is impeccable, the edges sharp, and it's well balanced."

Abaddon let out a heavy sigh. "This spectacle you're putting on is getting tedious. What is it you want, Evanora?"

A flash of anger crossed her sister's face, and she moved from behind the bar, her steps sharp as she quickly took up a position in front of their father.

Evanora placed the blade at Abaddon's heart. "What I want is revenge for what she did to me."

Selena froze as her sister pressed the blade deeper into her father's suit jacket. "I want her to hurt the same way she made me hurt when she took the only father I ever knew."

The corners of the Abaddon's lips quirked up at the side. "Well, go ahead then. Kill me and be done with it."

She jerked her hand away. "You didn't think it would be that easy, did you?"

She pointed the blade at Selena. "No. I want you to do it. Here is your choice. Either you kill your father, or you watch your beloved Shalik bleed out all over this barroom floor."

Selena glanced between her father and Shalik's wide, frightened eyes. "Remove his gag."

Evanora gave a brief nod to the demons holding Shalik. One held him still while the other cut the tie from around his mouth. Selena moved closer, lowering herself until they were eye to eye.

"Are you okay?"

"You know me. I like it rough sometimes."

Selena snorted. "You just couldn't help yourself, could you?"

"If I'm going to go out, then it might as well be with a smile."

Selena chewed on her bottom lip at his words. They were in a horrible predicament. No matter what she did, she was going to lose someone she cared about.

Shalik reached over and gripped her hands. "I didn't get to tell Mini before... But I love you, Lena, and no matter what happens, I'm at peace with it."

She fought back the tears that sprang to her eyes. Shalik had already accepted his fate, but she couldn't.

"We're going to get through this," she whispered.

"That's a very nice sentiment," Evanora cut in. "But time is ticking, and you have a choice to make."

Selena pushed to her feet, eyes hard, her magic gathering. "I refuse."

Evanora stepped closer so that she was within kissing distance. "What did you say?"

"I won't play your puppet games. You want me to kill one of them so you can get the satisfaction of revenge, but I won't give it to you. If you want them dead, do it yourself."

There was a manic look in her sister's eyes a split second before Selena felt the sharp sting of the celestial blade embedding into her side.

"Selena," Raesean screamed.

His voice sounded as though he was down a loud corridor, not standing next to her.

Selena wrapped her fingers around the blade in her side while her knees gave out. She didn't even feel the pain of connecting with the hard travertine floor as she crumpled.

"I've had enough of this." Abaddon released his magic, and the feeling of fear coated the room. Demons screamed, their hands going to their heads, yanking on their hair. Many curled in on themselves, falling to the floor like that was their only refuge.

"Release my soldiers," Evanora demanded, taking a step toward her father.

"You, who haven't even lived a couple of decades, think to come into the Underworld and rule it? Do you think it's that easy to keep some semblance of peace in the dark where beings only seek the destruction of everything good?"

Evanora ignored Abaddon, looking around at all the demons crying in terror. She called her magic, summoning sharpened pieces of reflective glass. They whistled through the air, cutting everything in their path.

Selena gritted her teeth as she pushed to her feet, calling for her own magic as a shield to protect her family. Raesean threw his flames, disintegrating the demons holding him and Shalik prisoner. The mirrors Evanora called halted as though embedded in a wall, shaking with the effort to move forward.

"You just won't let me have anything, will you?" Evanora gritted out as she tried to use her magic to force the shards forward. "You've always had everything, and now you want to take what's mine."

"No. You could have had everything you wanted. We would have welcomed you with open arms if you had only come with kindness. Instead, you came with force, so now you get nothing."

Her sister's gaze finally turned to Selena, locking onto the celestial weapon sticking out of her side. "Looks like you'll get your wish."

Selena knew what Evanora was going to do and yanked the blade out of her side with a soft scream before her sister could grab it.

Evanora's eyes widened as Selena advanced on her, lifting the blade.

It was as though time sped up and slowed down at the same moment. Selena quickly arced the blade down toward her sister, waiting to feel the satisfaction of the blade sliding home. At the last second, someone yanked Evanora out of the way, and the blade buried into the flesh of her father.

Time slowed, and Selena watched in horror as her father sucked in a painful breath. His hand wrapped around hers as she held onto the blade sticking out of his chest. His eyes locked with hers, and he gave her a small smile.

"I couldn't let you kill her, love. She's still my daughter, your sister. She just needs a little guidance."

Selena let out a loud wail when she realized what he'd done. He'd sacrificed himself for Evanora. The strength left his body, and he collapsed, taking Selena to the floor with him. "You're going to make a great queen. Keep Raesean, Shalik, and Cerberus with you always. They're the only ones you can trust."

"No, no, no. You're going to be fine. You can do this. I'm not ready to be queen. Stay awake, okay? I didn't..."

"I know you didn't mean for this to happen. It was my fault. My choice. I couldn't let you kill her."

Tears leaked down Selena's face. Her father's skin turned a molted gray, his eyes blinked slowly, and he called out for Raesean.

Raesean was by her father's side in seconds, gripping his hands. Selena didn't hear what they said to each other. All she could focus on was the fact that her father had opted to enter a hundred-year sleep so that her sister could live, and now the ungrateful bitch was lying on the floor laughing as her father closed his eyes for the last time in the next hundred years.

Chapter 28

Can a heart break twice?

Everything had crumbled in a matter of moments, and he didn't know how they'd gotten here.

Watching Selena slide the blade into her father's chest had chipped a piece of his off. The horror and pain on her face had shown him she'd realized her mistake immediately.

He looked on while she talked with her father, her eyes flashing the brown that he loved and the silver that showed her magic was close. She was holding herself together, but he didn't know for how long.

He heard Abaddon whisper his name, and he crawled over to spend the last moments with the king of the Underworld.

Raesean took the hand of the man who had saved his life in more ways than one.

"Stay with her, Raesean," Abaddon choked out. "She's going to need everything you have to give her."

Abaddon's words were bittersweet. To know that this man who'd saved him, treated him like one of his own, was entering a hundred-year sleep and leaving the one thing he valued above all else in his hands.

"You're good for her," Abaddon whispered. "And she's going to need that from you."

Raesean nodded, emotions choking any words he wanted to convey. "I'll see you in a hundred years... Son."

With those last words, Abaddon closed his eyes, and Raesean's heart squeezed. He was going to miss him. He would do right by him if it was the last thing he did.

High-pitched laughter cut into the moment he was having with his father, and Raesean looked over to the witch whom Abaddon had sacrificed himself for.

Evanora was pushing herself to her feet, her body shaking as she laughed at Abaddon's cooling body.

"I guess I got what I wanted." She looked around at the now-recovering demons in the room. Her smile was smug as she glanced at Selena. "With your father dead, all I need now is to take care of you, and the throne is mine."

"You think I would let you rule the Underworld?" Selena's voice rose an octave as she looked at her sister with hatred in her eyes. "I would rather call all the angels from Elysium to destroy this place than give you control."

"You're so dramatic," Evanora muttered, moving away from them. "Always making threats and promises you can't keep."

"Trust me, this one I will keep. You will never rule the Underworld."

"And how will you stop me?" Her heels clacked against the floor. "I'm in control of the army, and you need soldiers to keep a kingdom."

Selena let out a bitter laugh. "You're a child. You know nothing about this world. My father ruled this world since its inception. You only know this stupid bar."

Evanora gave Selena her manic smile, and Raesean knew what she would do next would irrevocably change everything.

"I may not know how to rule the Underworld, but I know one thing."

The air around them let out a sharp whistle, and the light bounced off the moving mirrors a second before they embedded into flesh with a thunk, thunk, thunk.

"I never let my emotions cloud the control of my magic." Raesean followed the direction Evanora was looking. His eyes widened, and he heard Selena's breath catch as she inched over to where Shalik's body lay slumped on the floor.

His blood was spreading over the disgusting bar room floor while his body lay unmoving. There was no sound in the room. It was as though every demon knew that disaster was to come.

Raesean watched as Selena looked down at her dead friend, her brother, and the last member of her family. She brushed the stray strands of his blue hair from his face. "Shalik," she whispered, giving his body a little shake as though she was hoping he would wake up and tease her the way he usually would.

Her fingers fisted in his blood-covered shirt and her scream broke the silence.

Could a heart break twice? Raesean didn't know, but he saw the exact moment Selena's heart turned to dust. It was when she looked down into Shalik's unseeing eyes.

The ground shook, the air vibrated, and Selena's eyes bled silver. The glow of her magic grew from the tips of her fingers and toes, traveling up her body until the silver-white light of her power took over the copper color.

Selena made a slow turn around the room. Every reflective surface in the room moved with her like a deathly dance of magic. Her silver eyes searched the room for her sister.

"Where is Evanora?" she asked. Her voice was unfamiliar, not the smooth, sultry tone he loved to hear speak his name, but a raspy octave that scratched over his skin, leaving goosebumps behind.

Selena moved forward, the once rebellious demons cowering in her presence. She curled her fingers, and the mirrors prodded the nearest demon forward. "Where is she?"

"She took a mirror portal out when you were calling your magic," he muttered, dropping to his knees before her.

"Please," he begged, "all we wanted was our freedom. We have families we care about, and all we wanted was for them to see the surface world. We didn't mean for this to happen."

Selena tsked. "And you shall have it."

"Thank you, my queen." He bowed his head.

Selena looked at the demon as he whispered his thanks to her feet.

"Is that how you all feel? You just wanted the freedom Evanora promised you?"

There were murmurs of agreement in the room, and Raesean wondered if the demons knew they were sealing their fate.

Silence filled the room for a few heartbeats before Selena moved to the doors that the demons had forced them to walk through. She looked out into the darkness for a moment before slamming it shut. The lock flipped with an ominous click before Selena turned back to the crowd. Her gaze took in the expression of every demon before her eyes finally landed on Raesean.

"You told me you would stand by my side whether I chose the light or the dark."

Raesean looked down at the sleeping king of the Underworld, then up at its new queen. He released the king's hand, gently laying it on his chest, then pushed to his feet.

He took a few steps toward her, placing his finger under her chin. He searched her eyes for any sign of the woman he'd met all those years ago. The carefree one that was now learning who she wanted to be, but she was gone, and in her place stood the darkness he'd seen in her.

Raesean laid his lips gently on hers. This kiss a physical promise that he would keep his word in the face of all they'd lost today. He would stand by her side, always.

"I once gave you up because I thought I had to choose the man who saved me over you. He may have saved me, but you taught me I could want more."

Raesean wiped an errant tear that tracked its way down her face, leaving a trail of mercury color behind.

"No matter what comes, I'll always choose you."

Selena nodded, turning back to the demon army that had helped take away everyone in her family except the one who stood by her side.

"Raesean?"

One look in her eyes and he knew what was coming. Selena yanked the red pendant off her necklace, using her magic to control the mirrors until it floated up above them.

"I don't need their bodies. Just their the souls to punish."

"As my queen commands."

Raesean called the hottest flames he could muster, releasing them onto the demons now trapped in the shitty bar they wanted freedom in.

They moved in sync, stepping forward to eliminate the hundreds of demons running for any exit they could find, cornering them like rats. Many tried pounding on the walls and windows, hoping to escape their fate; others tried digging holes in the ground or breaking doors and chairs to shield them.

It was useless—if the flames of Raesean's magic didn't get them, then the sharp slivers of Selena's did.

The demons' screams fueled Raesean's anger, and by the way Selena's skin kept glowing brighter, her magic was growing even stronger. Stronger with her own anger, stronger with every soul she collected in this filthy bar.

The glass from her pendant was glowing blood red above them, the various colored lights of souls streaming toward it as they were sucked in and trapped there. Most of their bodies turned to ash a split second before the pendant snatched up their souls, some a moment after.

When the last scream faded, and there was nothing but ash and the bodies of their loved ones, Selena called her pendant back to her. She clutched it in her hands, a satisfied smile on her face as though she could see the souls in there fighting to get out.

Maybe she could. He didn't know every facet of her magic—it was ever-changing, and he was sure it would change even more after tonight, after her magic claimed those souls, but he didn't care. They deserved whatever punishment she dished out.

"I want the rest of them," she murmured, reattaching the pendant to her necklace. "I want the rest of the demon army that turned on my father."

Raesean slid his hands into the pockets of his suit pants. "And you shall have them."

"And when I find my sister, I'll make sure she wishes she was never born."

"On that, we couldn't agree more."

As they stood on the ashes, blood, and excrement of the demons they had punished, he took her lips in a kiss hotter than the flames he used before. A kiss to seal their promise, to hunt down every being who sided with Belial and Evanora. Every being who caused her to lose her family.

His wrath was coming, and so was the darkness of her magic.

Evanora

Her sister had stolen her magic.

Well, some of it, anyway. If she hadn't hightailed it out of there, Selena would have surely taken it all. She hadn't known her sister could do that. No one ever said she could take someone's magic, and now, with their father dead, Evanora knew she had to escape the Abyss before her sister came looking for her.

She knew Selena wouldn't miss a second time. She still didn't know why Abaddon would try to save her, but she was glad for it. Now, she just had to escape and lie low until she could get rid of her sister and free the demons like Belial wanted.

This war between them wasn't over, and Evanora would do anything to get what she wanted. It was time she stepped up her own magic, and there was only one way to do that. To consult a mirror witch. One much stronger than her sister.

Epilogue

There was a demon screaming on the dance floor.

Not the screaming that said he was having a fabulous time at the club Valaria, but one that said he was in excruciating pain due to the owner of the club being very cross with him.

This would have disturbed Raesean, but it had become commonplace to hear some being or other screaming whenever Selena was on the lower level of her club. Raesean slid one hand into the pocket of his suit pants and searched the crowded room for his queen.

Music was pounding through the speakers, but no one dared to step onto the dance floor while the mirror witch was in a mood.

Raesean sighed. He wondered what had set her off this time.

"My vicious creature," he said, walking up to her side, careful of the slivers of mirror floating around the room. "Isn't it a little early in the evening to get demon blood on the dance floor?"

She turned mirror-colored eyes toward him, her skin glowing like the moonlight. "I wouldn't have had to get blood on the dance floor if this idiot hadn't insulted me twice."

Raesean reached out to pull her closer to him. Most times, when he had his hands on her, that temper of hers would calm down. As he'd hoped, she melted against him, the glow from her skin slowly diminishing, leaving the silver only in her eyes.

"And what did the demon do that warrants his torture and death?" he murmured, rubbing his lips softly against hers.

"See for yourself." Selena waved her hand toward an over-turned wicker basket that had scattered its contents all over the shiny dance floor.

Raesean set her aside, kneeling to pick up an item from the floor. "You're taking the life of the demon because he brought you vegetables?"

Selena huffed. "You make it sound like I was being unreasonable, but I'll have you know that I would have forgiven him for this offensive incident if he hadn't laid his hands on Pacco."

There it was.

He knew his queen was vicious and would slice a being into ribbons if they crossed the line, but they had to cross the line, and her hatred of vegetables wasn't a good enough reason to set her off. No, the laying of hands on Pacco, the young apprentice who worked in her club, was definitely the reason that set her off.

Raesean looked over at the demon curled up on the ground a foot away from him. It had bright blue hair, shaved on one side, that hung down past his shoulders. The honey-colored skin and brown eyes reminded him of someone whose name shall never be uttered in the presence of his queen, or heads will literally roll.

"Why did you touch the boy?" Raesean asked, carefully looking over the demon trembling under his gaze. Something about the demon wasn't adding up, and the one thing he didn't like was the unknown. Especially around Selena. It usually meant danger to her life, and he couldn't have that.

"He tried to stop me from speaking with the queen, and I got angry. I didn't mean to hit him that hard."

"I tried to stop the idiot from giving her the basket because I knew she was liable to flay his skin, and the ungrateful fool hit me. This is the thanks I get for trying to be nice," Pacco grumbled.

Raesean stole a glance at the young boy who was sporting a bruise on his cheek. Seeing the mark there reminded him of when he was young and helpless and collected his own from bigger demons. Maybe his queen had been right to slice the skin off of this demon, but again, something wasn't right.

"Who sent you?" Raesean asked. The setup was too perfect. The way he looked like Selena's dead best friend, that he attacked someone helpless, a pet peeve of Raesean's. Someone wanted to push their buttons, and he wanted to know who.

"I don't know what you mean," the demon responded.

Raesean called fire to his index finger, making it as hot as possible.

"I won't ask again." He lowered the flame to the demon's eye so that the heat singed his eyelashes.

The demon lifted his hands to ward off the attack, and several slices of mirror embedded into his hands, pinning them down. The demon screamed.

"Answer my question," he commanded.

The demon laughed. "You can't do shit. You're not the king of the Underworld, and once you burn me, my soul will return to Amaryllis."

"I see. Now I know who sent you." Raesean pushed to his feet. "She lied to you about your soul returning to Amaryllis to be reborn because your queen of the Underworld can take your soul right out of your body and keep it trapped and screaming in one of her mirrors."

The demon's eyes widened. "You're lying."

"Why would I lie about your future?"

The demon struggled to free himself from where he was impaled.

"You have one chance to escape your fate," Raesean warned. "Tell us where Evanora is, and I'll give you a quick death."

"I... I... I don't know," the demon stammered.

"Right. Good luck with the whole soul in the mirror thing."

A two-inch shard of mirror floated over the demon.

"Pacco, why don't you head to the back and mix some potions or something?" Selena murmured, her skin already glowing.

"No, I'm good," Pacco said.

"It wasn't a question, Pacco."

"Fine," the kid muttered, stomping off to the back room.

"Now, where was I." Selena looked down at the demon who'd pissed himself after he got a look at Selena.

She chanted a spell in the old demonic language, and the mirror above the demon glowed.

"Wait. I'll tell you," he screamed.

"We're waiting," Raesean said.

"She's in the south human lands."

"Thank you." Raesean tossed a spark on the demon, and he went up like dry kindling. The demon screeched long and loud, even as Selena yanked his soul into her mirror.

"What have you done?"

Raesean looked up into the horrified face of Reuel. The angel's wings fluttered as he tucked them away, his eyes looking down at the flaming body at their feet.

"Selena," he whispered. "What... How?"

"I'm just going to keep his soul until I find my sister. Just to make sure he wasn't lying. Then he can return to Amaryllis."

The angel looked like he was about to be sick, and Raesean fought to keep the smug satisfaction off of his face. It was a struggle.

"What brings you to Fusion City, Reuel? This isn't your normal stomping grounds."

He looked at Raesean, and anger filled his eyes. "I came to deliver a message. You've made some changes to the Underworld, and the higher-ups aren't pleased. They want you to run things the way your father did."

Selena grabbed the mirror out of the air before moving closer to Reuel.

"Tell me. Do angels have souls?"

What happens when Selena, the mirror witch, hunts down her sister to enact her revenge and face off with the angels of Elysium with our favorite demon at her side? Find out in book three.

More from D.H. Gibbs

Mirror Witch Magic

Lost Thrones Series

Crown By Blood (Free Prequel)

Queen By Blood (Book 1)

Alpha by Blood (Book 2)

Heir by Blood (Book 3)

Kidnapped and taken to a secret island where Nika's forced to give up the freedom she desperately wants to protect a race on the brink of extinction. Made extinct by the brother she didn't know she had. As the immortal queen, she has no choice but to take her brother's life and claim all the thrones if he doesn't kill her first. Who will survive the fight between the siblings? Or will their rivalry lead to the very war their mother tried to avoid centuries ago?

About the author

D.H. Gibbs is a USA Today Bestselling Author and Newsday T&T Choice finalist. She enjoys writing fantasy, contemporary romance, and children's books. When not navigating the adventures of her kick-ass female leads, she's a complete Starbucks and book addict who binge-watches TV series like Lucifer, Carnival Row, and Warrior. A Trinidadian native, she currently lives and creates new worlds in Japan.

For exclusive reads, updates and sneak peeks about her real-life shenanigans, subscribe to her newsletter.
https://dhgibbs.com/newsletters/

Scan QR code to grab my links